Contents

Age 40, Just Arrived in Key West	1
Red's Early Fishing Days	10
Bud's First Fishing Job & First Charter	17
Bud's Early Experience on Other Boats	29
Vance Comes to Key West/Tennacious	34
Leasing the Danny III	40
Fun Trip/Vance, Kit, & I on the Miss Gina	45
Michael Lewis & Bald Faced Liar Joke	52
Derrick & Drunk Front	53
Carol & Bud Meet & Purchase the Miss Gina	58
Lady With the Tube Top on Miss Gina	63
Victor is Hired & Sick Boy Catches Sailfish	71
Blondel Hancock Commercial Fishing	80
Naked Charter on the Miss Gina with Kit & Victor	86
Art Cole & Six Sailfish Day	90
Funeral At Sea	92
Derelict Boat Towing	95
Carol's Dad Dies, Feb., '91	101
Suicide Attempt, Stuart is the Mate	104
Fun Trip on Cha Cha	108
Purchase of Ms. Gina	114

Fun Trip/Ms. Gina to Boca Grande	118
Red's Sea Adventures/Talking to Vance & Bud	123
Ms. Gina Picks Up Scuba Diver/Victor is Mate	136
Conch Tour of Key West & Changing Oil	140
Dry Tortugas Trip on Ms. Gina	144
BASTA/First Trip to Cuba	148
Victor & Voodoo Charter	157
Mr. Garcia & Son/Trip to Cay Sal Ban	163
Good Bye to the Captain	174
Key West Changed and So Did I	178
Glossary	190
Maps and Diagrams	198

Acknowledgements

I wish to thank all the people who helped to edit this book. My special thanks goes to Carol, who has been my right hand. She has encouraged me and has patiently helped me with the pictures, maps, and memories. This book is dedicated to her with love, respect, and gratitude. I also want to thank the other editors: Bob Emmons, Sue Rogers, Sudye Cauthen, Boots and John Vassar, and Jim Morris.

Captain Bud Williams

Chapter 1.
Age 40, Just Arriving in Key West

Yes, this is all about me.

Now day's people say, "Well, is this all about you?"

Again, yes.

I was driving the one hundred fifty-seven miles of two lane road from Miami to Key West. As I passed over the seven-mile bridge, I looked at the water on both sides. It was aqua green. The sky was pale blue in the background. White puffy clouds formed small animals. The air was fresh and clean, with a smell of salt and sea weed.

As I drove, I thought about the times when I was a small boy going with the adults to see my dad. My mother told me he was a fisherman in Key West, Fla. They got divorced after WW II, when I was three.

We would stop at a bar at the start of the Keys, The Last Chance Saloon. It is still there. After they drank--as they said "a couple of beers"--we continued on to the next watering hole. I sat on the floor boards of the rear seat with three adults' feet kicking me. These adults were a group mostly made up of relatives. Sometimes a friend or two would join them. Aunt Edna, her husband Uncle Jim, Aunt Myrtle, her husband Uncle Mike, my mother Bee, and others that were nameless to me. The ladies always wore sun dresses, slips, and high heeled shoes. The men had flowered shirts, slacks, hard toed leather shoes, and straw hats to ward off the sun. We were riding in a ten to twelve year old Dodge. All four windows were open. There was no air conditioning in those days. The heat wasn't too bad as long as the car was moving at the speed limit.

Sitting there on the floor I kept getting kicked. I thought it was not for something I had done, but for something I might do in the future. From my point of view, I could see six fat legs, hear lots of talk, and listen to Johnny Cash singing on the AM single speaker radio. I would watch the telephone poles with a cross bar at the top carrying four wires. Occasionally, I got comfortable and would nod off to sleep. That would help to pass the time. The Tollgate Inn was one of the stops on the road. It's now Bahia Honda State Park. The old two lane road and bridge is still there but the Inn is long since gone. While the adults took a pit stop, I stayed outside to stretch my legs and see what I could discover. In the back of the bar and restaurant there was a white sand beach and a boat dock for small skiffs. The water was as clear as drinking water. I saw my first shark. I suppose it was a small three foot sand shark. There were also some black and yellow sergeant majors and four small yellow tails. If I only had a hook and line, I would have started my fishing career thirty years earlier.

It's a hundred and fifty-seven miles from Miami to Key West. It takes about three and a half hours to drive the distance if one doesn't stop for refreshments, whatever they may be.

A first timer should stop along the way to see the Coral Castle, the fishing marinas, and other marine attractions, as well as at the Green Turtle Inn for a cup of turtle soup.

We would arrive in Key West about dark, go downtown to Duvall Street, check in at Sloppy Joe's. They asked for Red Williams. In a small town like Key West, the locals are known to each other. Nevertheless, no one knew where he was, not even to a small child. But of course, we may as well have a beer, and me, my fourth coke. As the saying goes, you can't walk on one leg, so you have to have another.

Next stop, the charter boats. Me, being the youngest, I would go ask the fishermen if they had seen Red. NO, NO, NO, but somehow we always found him.

After I went to college on a football scholarship to Harden Simmons College in Texas, got married, had two kids, and got divorced, I was at the age that I wanted to know more about this type of life. My mother and her sisters had told me stories about Red and the other men they met on their trips to Key West.

I wasn't sure what to expect, but I knew their stories of a carefree life of fishing, drinking, and womanizing and I was eager to become a part of that excitement and to get to know my father after so many years. I was filled with anticipation. I really wanted to see what the fishing boat life was all about.

I knew a few store owners from past years, plus my dad had been working at the same bar for the last seventeen years. Now he was night watchman, cleaner, and bouncer. He became tired of going to sea after forty-five years. He knew the Ramos family that owned a lot of properties. They gave him a lifetime job at a restaurant and bar called Delmonico's.

Delmonico's was located in the two hundred block of Duvall Street. That means it's two blocks from the waters of the Gulf of Mexico. They had five separate bars. Directly inside the two large front doors of the white stucco building there was a disco with a live DJ that played loud music at night. Upstairs there was a piano bar with a mostly gay clientele. A small Tike bar was located outside in the landscaped back garden. A separate building held the Taco bar that was frequented by women. Outside this building the Patio bar was decorated with white gravel, palm trees, and metal tables and chairs. At night when the disco would crank up, the crowd included the local fishermen and merchants, the military stationed in Key West, the gays who lived and visited the area, the tourists visiting the island, and the drug dealers peddling to everyone.

We arrived downtown, and went to Delmonico's to find Red. The years at sea had made his skin rough and wrinkled. He had deep lines in his face. His hair was snow white. His skin color was white from working years at night. He said he had been working at that bar for seventeen years with seven different owners. People would lease the place from the Ramos family, but would get caught up in the booze, drugs, partying, and go broke.

Next!

So much for now. What about yesterday? Red, the captain, was born in 1909 in Key West, FL, a small sea town. The fishermen gathered sea turtles, lobster, sponges, and fish. He went to sea as a fireman at sixteen on a ship called the *Governor Cobb*. He stoked the fire box with a shovel all day. Hot, hard work for a man that was five feet six inches, one hundred thirty-five pounds.

During his years on the ship, he learned navigation and piloting. Then he got his captain's license. Local people who owned boats always needed a good captain.

He got a boat, the *Evalynn*, which he kept docked on Front Street. They called it Front Street because it was at the edge of the water. At that time, the late twenties, early thirties, some tourist would come to town and hire a boat, captain, and mate. These people, mostly men, wanted to catch the big one, like in the movie, <u>To Have and To Have Not</u>, with Humphrey Bogart. As captain of a charter boat, my father's most famous charter was Ernest Hemingway. Before Ernest bought the *Pilar*, Red would take him out several times a week.

I've told these stories throughout the years. Everyone wants to hear about Ernest Hemingway. He came to Key West in the early thirties. I was born in 1942, so Earnest had left town long before I got there. My father said little about Hemingway except that he was a big man and a heavy drinker at that time.

Charter boats were few in those days. At the Front Street docks there were only three or four boats. Two boats were docked at the Casa Marina Hotel on the South side of the island. There was a total of nine charter boats in Key West.

The north side of the island of Key West faces the Gulf of Mexico, and the south side of the island the Atlantic Ocean. Each body of water has its own peculiarity. The Gulf of Mexico has shallow water. Going north out of the North West Channel twenty miles you're still in twenty to thirty feet of water. This is where you can catch lobster, crabs, snapper, and sponges. The Atlantic, on the south side stays shallow only for a short distance, about 7 miles. Then it drops quickly to one hundred feet, then two hundred feet, etc. Eighteen miles out, the water is one thousand feet deep.

One day Ernest came to get Red. He told him to get the boat ready, because they were going fishing. Red did the necessary things.

When Earnest got to the boat, he and his wife were yelling and arguing. Red cast off the lines and away he and Ernest went, leaving the angry woman behind.

Red put the lines out and trolled around for a while. Earnest said to bring the lines in and set a course for Havana, Cuba. The man was paying him, so off they went.

In those days the only navigational aid he had was a compass. Pointing the boat SE, it's ninety miles from Key West to Havana. They were already ten miles out, so they only had eighty miles to go. When making this crossing, it was possible to fish along the way. I've done this myself.

The small single gasoline engine on the *Evalynn* traveled at ten or eleven knots, so it was an all day trip. They also were fighting the gulf stream which is a river of water that runs in a northerly direction at 3 to 5 knots thru the Florida Straits, the body of water between Key West and Cuba.

After arriving in Cuba, Ernest went about his business. He had a house there. My father didn't have any extra clothes, money, or anything. They stayed a week or ten days, but Hemingway didn't care about Red, or his problems. Once in a while they fished off the reef, but other than that, Red waited. There are only so many things to do to the boat--clean, repair, check the engines, rods, and reels. Then they came back to Key West when Hemingway was ready.

On the reverse trip you take a reciprocal course. This is the opposite course that you took to start with. This time the gulf stream is helping you so the trip is only about six hours. They took some time out to catch the occasional dolphin or tuna.

Chapter 2.
Red's Early Fishing Days

Evalynn was Red's first memorable charter boat. He took care of the repairs, cleaning, painting, tackle, and taking tourists out to fish. It was owned by a doctor in town that only came to the boat every two weeks or once a month. When he came he collected the money and receipts. The charter trips at that time cost fifty dollars for the day.

Red told me one time he needed to clean the bottom so he went to the dry dock to pull the boat out of the water on the railroad tracks. To do this, the boat would sit on a platform on the tracks and was rolled up onto dry land. The owner said it would cost thirty-five dollars to be hauled out this way. Red said, "Hell, No, that's way too much money!" He took the boat to a sand bar where he threw out two anchors to hold the boat in the shallows. He then waited six hours for the tide to go down. The boat tilted to one side as the tide went out and he scraped and painted that side of the bottom. He waited for the next cycle of the high and low tide and scraped and painted the other side. The waiting time for the tide to come in allowed the paint to dry, so in 24 hours he had cleaned and painted the whole bottom and saved thirty-five dollars. It was a lot of work but he would have had to do the scraping and painting anyway even if he had the lift pull the boat out of the water.

In the spring, summer, and fall, Captain Red would take people out on charters. He would get some food, a case of different kinds of drinks, including booze, and away they would go. It must have been great to fish with one or two people. In those days, they had no pollution and a lot more fish than in today's waters.

My father fished commercially in the winter. During January and February, fishing for king mackerel you could make good money if you went alone. Mates weren't worth a damn and you had to pay them. So, he would go alone. You go find a school, put two lines out on the same side of the boat, one high off the top using a clothes pin to hold the line, the other off the back corner of the stern with a clothes pin. No bait was needed. A shiny spoon with a sharp hook was used. The boat was steered around in a circle, spoons on the inside. When a strike happens, the line would get tight and snap loose. Now the work starts. This five foot six inch, one hundred thirty-five pound man would pull in these fighters that weighted from ten to thirty pounds. You repeat this scenario until you can't do it any longer, or the school leaves or stops biting.

There were times when he caught two thousand pounds of king fish at eight cents a pound. Now that's a good day. By the time you pay the owner, pay the fuel, food, drink, etc., little was left. As the Cubans say "mucho travjo, poquito dinero" (lots of work, little money).

A fisherman is up at first light, checking the water, fuel, oil, getting bait, and ice to keep the fish fresh after they are caught. Then he goes out to fish. When the fishing is done, he still has to drive the boat to the fish house, gut the catch, unload, collect the money, and return to the dock. Now, with what was left of the day, it would be time for beer and there was a bar conveniently across the street. We can let the washing of the boat wait for a while!

These kinds of trips were done by a lot of fishermen during the thirties and forties, and even today.

My Uncle Picky told me he did trips like this during the second World War. When going out and returning, he had to dodge the military patrol boats. The government told everyone when, where, and what they could do. You had to make a living, so this is what they had to do to fish.

I first met Picky in 1983 before I started my own fishing career. I was working as a bouncer and night watchman at a bar called Michael's. It was the same bar Red had worked in when it had been named Delmonico's and was still working at with the new name. Red had gotten sick, too sick to work, so I had taken his place while he recovered.

I stayed after the four a.m. closing until eight o'clock in the morning, when one of the owners would come to relieve me. At that time of the morning Key West is a ghost town. Only a few people would be cleaning up the bars and the streets after the night's partiers had gone home.

I would gather some bait and my rods and head to Pier 3 for a while. Pier 3 was not used much for ship docking, so a lot of locals used it for fishing. It is one of the three piers at Key West's harbor. Several old timers came in the morning, especially if the tide was coming in.

I found fishing to be a wonderful way to meet people who could help me learn, since I was a novice at this type of fishing. I would ask what kind of bait to use, or what size hook would work best. Picky would give me fishing tips and would talk about the old days in Key West, the boats, the war(WWII), and the many interesting adventures he had then. I told him that I worked at Michael's with my dad, Red Williams.

His response surprised me. He said he knew that white haired old man who walked with a limp. He said, "That's my cousin!" Picky and I were second cousins and neither of us knew it before that moment.

My Grandfather, Captain Red's dad, came to Key West from Wales during the wreckers days of 1880. Grandfather Guy Williams worked at the boating trade also, sometimes a land job, sometimes a sea job.

My dad said little about his father, because he actually knew very little about him. It is hard to pick an old man's head about something he doesn't want to talk about. I did find out that Guy was not home much when Red was growing up, sometimes taking trips to Georgia that lasted several weeks.

Guy Williams married into the Marshall family in the early 1900's. The Marshals had come to the Keys from the Bahamas prior to

1900. Guy and my grandmother had five children. Captain Red was the middle child.

Red told me where my grandfather and grandmother were buried in the Key West cemetery and the house he died in. It is a small frame Conch house across the street from the electric power plant.

Just to fill in a little history of early Key West, on May 15, 1513, Antonio DeHerrere gave the keys the original name of Los Martires (the martyrs), because the rocks appeared like men who were suffering. For many years the islands were left to the pirates. The deep water port attracted names like Blackbeard and Jean LaFitt who stopped there for safe haven.

In 1815, Don Juan de Estrada of Spain granted Key West or Cayo Huese (island of bones) to Juan Pablo Salas for meritorious service to the crown. It was named the island of bones because so many bones were found by these inhabitants.

John W. Simonton of Alabama, bought the island from Salas for two thousand dollars in 1821. For many years wrecking and salvaging became a principal occupation of the islanders. They salvaged the goods from the ships that floundered on the nearby reef. Some say the wreckers deliberately lured ships onto the shoals. There are stories of people bribing the lighthouse keep to turn the light off as a ship would approach the reef. The ship would crash on the coral. Everyone who had a boat would set sail to gather the loot from the wrecked ship and sell it on shore. This practice made Key West the richest city per capita in the United States in the late eighteen hundreds.

Chapter 3.
Bud's First Fishing Job & First Charter

I've talked to people through the years who said, I wish I would have done this or that. Well, I'm here in Key West, my dad works nights at a bar. He lives next door and has an extra room for me. Now what's wrong with that?

I had some money, but not much. Days I would go to The Bull, a corner bar. They played live, loud music.

Trying to get a job of some kind, I met a lot of locals. Telling them who my father was helped a lot and I got part time work as a laborer, helper, and so on.

My dad and I would sit on the porch upstairs and watch the people go up and down Duvall Street. There was my favorite speed bump just down below us. Girls on their bicycles would run over the bump and their tits would jump up and down. The more beer I drank, the better I liked it. I asked several girls to go around and do it again. They all said NO !!

After a few weeks of drinking, and sleeping late, Red told me to go to the docks and see a man called John Blackwell. He might show me what I needed to know about sport fishing, if he needed help.

To get a job as a mate on a sport fishing boat, there are a lot of things you need to know- how to tie wire, how to take apart a reel, sharpen a hook, get the boat ready to go before the customers get there, how to book the boat, what prices to charge for half day and full day trips, night shark trips, tarpon trips, and filleting all types of fish.

I saw John, and he did need a mate, but first a lot of work needed to be done on the charter boat *Carol*. So I was ready to learn, and eager to do it. Questions like, "How much does it pay?" were answered by, "Nothing till the boat is ready". The mate takes care of the boat. We had fourteen oil leaks in the two 453 Detroit engines. We sanded and painted the deck, sanded and varnished the bright work and repaired broken reels. After ten days of this type of work, I told John I couldn't work for nothing. I had to eat. I stayed with Red for nothing but I needed some money. He gave me one hundred twenty-five dollars a week.

Soon the *Carol* was ready, but we had no captain. I stayed behind the boat and talked to everyone that came by. A nice couple from Canada booked the boat for the next day. They were in their mid forties. Both had never missed a meal. It looked to me like it wouldn't hurt them to loose a few pounds.. He was wearing shorts and sneakers and one of those flowered shirts with hibiscus all over it that the tourists love so much. She was wearing white shorts and a white boat neck top. I explained that tomorrow she probably should not wear white on the fishing trip because when I gaff the fish they would flip back and forth and spray blood everywhere for a short time until I get it into the fish box. I also advised them not to wear expensive jewelry because if your hands get wet rings and watches might slide off and fall overboard and it will be gone forever.

I told John that I had a deposit for an all-day trip.

The next morning a captain showed up. His name was Michael Lewis. He did free lance captain work for a lot of boats at the dock.

I needed to get some wire leaders tied for the trip, at least two dozen. Jimmy Mantz, the mate on the next boat, *the Amorous,* made up a few. Big Gene, a mate from another boat, happened by so he tied a few. Captain Michael tied some.

Now the boat is ready. The reels are OK, not new, but OK. Wire leaders are made. They did teach me how to put the bait, a ballyhoo, on the hook. Ballyhoo are small cigar shaped fish with the bill on the bottom jaw. If you didn't get it just right, the bait would not swim correctly. It would spin and not look natural.

At eight o'clock the people arrived. I stowed their gear and helped them step on board. Most of the time, the charters are excited about trying a new venture, but now the captain and mate don't have time to chat. Now it's all business. The captain controls the boat while the mate casts off the stern lines as the boat is held in place with the reverse thrust of the engines. The mate then makes his way along the side of the boat to the bow to cast the two bow lines away far enough to stay away from the props. On the way out, there is a bridge, a couple of turns, then past the navy officers housing, and another bridge before you enter Key West harbor. We pass several hotels and dockside bars. Once we pass the Ocean Key House Hotel you have gone from the Gulf of Mexico into the Atlantic Ocean. You are now in open water. It is up with the outriggers, bolt down the deep troll, and hook on the twelve pound lead ball. By this time you have cleared the harbor and water is flying from the spray of the bow hitting the waves. It takes about forty-five minutes to get to the reef from the dock. From the island to the reef is seven miles of water that is only twenty to thirty feet deep. It is as clear as glass, but at the edge of the harbor when the wind goes against the tide, the waves get up. It's the worst place. From there on out it's not too bad if the wind doesn't get over fifteen knots. More than that you have got white caps in the bait bucket.

By this time, the people are gathered inside the cabin predicting who is going to catch the biggest, most, etc. Occasionally, one of the group says, "No, the mate is going to catch all the fish, and we are only going to reel them in." In the next twenty to thirty minutes the mate answers questions such as what is going to happen, how the rods are set up, what that thing is with the ball on it (deep troll), which direction we are going, how long I have been doing this, and are those islands to the west of us there all year round?

There are always lots and lots of questions. One lady wanted to get a sample of the different colors of water. The water color appears to change such as dark areas appearing under clouds or grass on the bottom. Light areas could be from light sandy bottom.

Well, passengers (or, as we referred to them "the charter") have been given the instructions. They ask a lot of questions, and hear a lot of answers, none of which they will remember when it comes time to take the rod and turn the handle clockwise.

Now it's my time to enjoy what I'm out here for. Every day is different people, different wind speed, different wind direction, different kinds of fish-winter, spring, summer, and fall.

The season started at Christmas for us.

On this small island in the gulf stream, if the temperature has been cold up north, we mostly caught king mackerel in the winter. Fish go south, just like the people and birds. Spring got a little warmer and we fished the reef on half day trips. We would go south to deeper water, looking for sailfish, dolphin, and wahoo on all-day trips.

Because I started in the winter, this trip we would be looking for king mackerel, tuna, barracuda, and whatever. By standing on the flying bridge, Michael and I could see for a long way. The Captain and mate take this fishing stuff seriously. Looking for birds flying in a bunch, staying in the same area, means the birds are feeding on small bait fish such as mahooa, sardines, or piltchers. Also, while standing on the bridge, different kinds of performances take place, such as dolphin playing. We call dolphin porpoise because there is a dolphin fish-it's not a mammal.

On a full day trip (eight hours) radio (VHF) contact is made with other boats, mainly charter vessels. We preferred to talk to guys who would give us a straight answer, and not lie to us about fishing conditions.

In Key West and the Florida Keys, is the only living reef in the continental United States. It runs east and west from Key Largo to the Dry Tortugas (sixty miles west of Key West). A lot of tourists come to the Keys for snorkeling, scuba diving, and fishing. The coral reef is a living entity. As well as coral, it has sea fans, sponges, etc. The fish gather along the reef for food and protection. The big fish eat the smaller ones. At the time I was doing this, we used the Loran and a compass to navigate. So, should we go east or west? That was always the question. Captain Michael contacted someone he knew on the VHF radio and decided to go east.

To break the ice, he cruised slowly by the nine foot stake (a pole at a place on the reef to indicate shallow water, nine feet deep at high tide). The reason being, the water is clear and people like to be entertained. I asked them to look over the side. It's like having a salt water aquarium under the boat. There are plenty of different kinds of fish swimming. We see a group of sergeant majors in a school of ten or twelve. These fish look like angel fish, flat and round with yellow and black stripes. Small yellow tails are darting back and forth. They have florescent yellow stripes along their midsection including the tail. There are great schools of twenty-five to fifty fish. When they get to three pounds, they are great eating. I would say this because all that people want to know is, can you eat this or that?

In the shallow water we got a little action from barracuda, yellow tail, and grouper on the deep troll, going slowly with the lead ball close to the bottom. On the flat line rod, I put a small yellow buck tail and set another hook with filet of ballyhoo, which runs out from the left hand side of the stern.

I've often forgotten, is this a fishing trip or a fishing lesson? Well, it's all the same to me. If people don't know what's going on, they can't catch them. If they don't catch fish, I get no tip. That is part of the game.

A few yellow tails were retrieved from the flat line. We got some strikes on the deep troll, to no avail. A cuda or two are caught on the outrigger. (Cuda is short for barracuda.)

This set the mood right. Now we would go looking for the bigger stuff--king fish, tuna, bonita, wahoo, and whatever! It depends on the time of year as to what to do next. In the winter, we might troll along the reef's edge where the bottom drops off to eighty feet or troll just outside the bar. The bar is a shallow strip that runs outside the reef.

A note: the reef fish stay in and around the reef. The other fish don't. They are called pelagic. Pelagic fish move according to the temperature of the water and the abundance of small bait fish.

Someone told me that they saw large tuna inside the reef where the water is shallow (twenty to thirty feet). Yellow fin tuna weigh seventy-five to one hundred fifty pounds...too big for such shallow water. Curious about this, on another occasion, I asked the captain, my father, if this could be true. He said, "They have tails. They can go anywhere they want to."

Michael heard someone on the radio reporting that black fin tuna were surfacing east of us, not too far away. We trolled in that direction. As the mate, now it is time for me to change the rigs for tuna.

Tuna like the bait to move at a faster speed and sort of skip along the surface of the water. Michael told me he wanted feathers on the outriggers, so I reeled in the present bait and snapped on new ones. When tunas come up to feed, the boat circles the school. This action doesn't drive down the fish; they stay on top of the water allowing more time to catch as many as you can before they move on. The inexperienced or unknowledgeable captain will steer the boat through the middle of the school, catching one and driving the rest down deep. We caught three or four and a couple of bonita.

After catching the fish, it's time for me to start cleaning up. Tunas and bonitas are bloody. When the mate gaffs the fish, it wiggles and sprinkles blood in all directions. Get out the water, hose, or bucket, and wash down the deck and the people's feet if they don't move. About this time, everyone wants to see what they have caught. "What kind is that? Is this a good day's catch?"

An aside here: If you go fishing, or have been fishing on a charter, or with a friend, it's not about the fish, it's about having fun, just like all things in life. For example, when people go to the park with friends, it's the joy of getting out of the routine. Now is the time to enjoy everything that is happening, like the sky, the breeze in your face, even the big one that got away. If you didn't catch him, he wasn't yours so he didn't really get away.

At last the boat is clean. The people are happy. Michael, the captain is happy. If I got paid and had a good tip, I am happy, also. That meant that I did a good job, and that was important.

On the way back in to the harbor, I went up on the fly bridge and chatted with the captain. I told him another captain had refused to take this trip because I was a non-fishing mate, meaning I had never been out before. He said, "not to worry, you were born to it."

So I fished the *Carol*. Blackwell's boat is a number one hull, thirty-nine feet in length, twin 453 Detroit engines, with a flat bottom, and small keel. This type of boat was built in Key West by Conchs. (Conchs are people born and raised in Key West.) For a few months, I learned what several free lance captains could teach me, including Blackwell. Blackwell hired a full time captain that did not like me. I felt from the start Poncho, the new captain and I both had strong personalities. He was suddenly in charge of the boat and I had gotten it going again after weeks of free labor. It was evident after a few trips together we would part company sooner or later. He wanted another mate he was familiar with. Being fired from my first boat, after I had cleaned, painted, and repaired her was disappointing. I was told that you can't run a boat without a captain, but you could run one without a mate. So, I was off to find a job.

Chapter 4.
Bud's Early Experience On Other Boats

I hooked up with a guy from New Jersey who ran a boat for the owner of a company called Tropical Fish Hobbyist, thus the name of the boat, *T.F.H.*. This captain liked to use light tackle, twenty pound and thirty pound test line. Light line blows in the wind like spider webs and tangles easily. Using light tackle and light rods and reels is all together different from the heavier fifty pound test line, rods and reels I was used to. The angler can't winch the fish in. He has to use more finesse and patience or the line will break. The most important part of setting up light tackle, twenty pound test for example, is setting the drag light so if the fish takes off at a high rate of speed the line won't snap. The drag is a clutch system on the side of the reel that loosens or tightens the line as it comes out of the spool. Turning the clutch clockwise tightens the line, counter clockwise loosens the drag on the line. If the drag is set too light the fish can't be stopped or slowed down with little or nothing pulling against him. There is nothing to tire the fish out.

One day we got a charter with two men, a father and son. The father was about sixty and the son thirty. We had been fishing for a while when a sailfish came up on the flat line. I dropped back and counted to three--one thousand one, one thousand two, one thousand three. By this time, the pointed-nosed creature had time to circle around and swallow the bait whole, head first. Sailfish have no teeth, so they swat the prey with their bills to disable it. Then they swallow it head first, whole. Then I raised the rod up and back to set the hook. He was caught. As soon as they feel the hook, out of the water they jump. Now it's time for me to give the rod to the son. It had already been predetermined he would catch the first fish. It happened to be this sailfish. I had to keep the line tight and move back to his chair, insert the rod in the gimble in the front and under the angler's chair. Then it's up to him. This man had fished several times before. He knew how to handle the rod. Pull back and wind down, over and over again till the fish gets to the boat, which took about twenty to twenty-five minutes. I grabbed the long nose with my left hand, gaffed with my right hand, and lifted it up on the deck and shoved the tail into the corner. I bent his head back. It quit fighting immediately. Then a swat to the head with a bat and it's over.

What makes this trip stand out in my mind is several things. It was the first time I ever used light line, and the first father-son team. The dad also caught a sailfish.

I worked several trips on the *T.F.H.* And learned a lot about light tackle.

Now it was on to the next boat. If I could work on a lot of boats with several different captains, it would be a great education, and so it was.

Charter boat row is located at the Key West City Marina which is at Garrison Bight (A bight is a body of water surrounded by land on three sides. It has an outlet to the sea or a larger body of water.) At the City Marina, the Port and Transit Authority is the land lord. The dockmaster is in charge of maintaining the facility as well as overseeing any construction, painting, plumbing, electric, and delegating slips to transient vessels passing through spending a few days or weeks in Key West. He also collects fees for using the boat ramp and enforces the marina rules and regulations.

At the charter boat docks there are about thirty fishing vessels. They range from small boats for light tackle fishing to very large boats that take up to sixty-five people bottom fishing for snappers and other pan fish for eating. All the boats take four hour, half day trips or eight hour, full day trips. The remainder of the marina, about eighty slips, is rented to people who live aboard their boats.

It is not unusual for boys to start out washing their father's boats and eventually take over the business. Johnny Potter and his father, Anthony Saldono and his father, and my father all fished off this dock in the fifties and sixties. The fathers have retired but the sons are still fishing. These two young captains taught me a lot about fishing in these waters around Key West.

In the waters off Key West there are coral rocks and reef wrecks. If a captain does not have the knowledge of these things, he can't catch fish.

After a year to year and a half training, a mate can begin to understand what is going on at each time of year. Spring-it's this fish and that place, summer-go deep and look for weed lines and dolphin (the fish-not the mammal). During my journey through apprenticeship I learned my trade well. This included booking the boat, catching the fish, filleting the fish, and selling the fish to the market or restaurant, whoever gave the best prices.

Chaprter 5.
Vance Comes To Key West/Tennacious

My son, Vance was in his mid twenties living in West Texas with his mother and sister who was a student at Texas Tech. He had been to several colleges with no interest in education. While working in the oil fields, he had a mishap that crushed both his feet. Now that his casts were off, I suggested he come to Key West and spend some time with me and his grandfather.

A few weeks passed before he got there. We set him up in our spare room. Ed, a friend of mine and I bought some used furniture-chair, couch, and table. Cheap was the name of the game; whatever we could beg or borrow. Most important of all was the eighteen cubic foot refrigerator that was furnished with the house. That's where we kept the beer.

The first thing all newcomers do when they get to Key West is catch the Key's Disease: drink to excess, stay out late, and chase girls. Vance was no different, so it was my job to show him how to do it right.

The Bull sits on the corner of Caroline and Duvall Streets, the main drag. It has no windows, just shutters, live music, cold beer, and tourists walking past. Did I mention that it stays open till 4 A.M. Or till you had enough, whichever comes first? Another bar is Che Che's. This is a real professional drinker's place. They are open from 9 A.M. Till 4 A.M. With hours like this it's possible to get drunk three times in one day.

I was told by my father, Captain Red, that Ernest Hemingway went to a bar on Green Street that used to be Sloppy Joe's. That bar today is called Captain Tony's. In the thirties, Joe Russel, the owner of Sloppy's, was renting the place from someone that raised the rent a few dollars. Joe got mad and rented another building on the corner of Duval and Green Streets. This place is the present Sloppy Joe's. The day the move was made Joe came into the bar and told everyone the place was closing and he was moving. Everyone picked up their drinks and walked the half block to the new building. Not a round was missed. Ernest later that day, on his way home, took a urinal from the old place to his house. It's only a three block walk. The urinal was used as a water fountain for the cats.

Sloppy Joe's was a favorite watering hole for Hemingway as well as my dad when he had a few dollars in his pocket. It was said every time Ernest came into Sloppy's he would buy the house a round. This sounds like a big deal but in the thirties the Depression was on and no one had money so there would only be three or four people in the bar and draft beer was only twenty-five cents.

The original Sloppy Joe's is now called Captain Tony's. The story goes, and it is only a story, that Captain Tony came to Key West in the fifties from New Jersey. He lived in his car for a while. He brought some money with him and put a down payment on a large bottom fishing boat. He had no license to operate the vessel, so he hired Captain Red to run the boat. He helped Tony get his captain's license and taught him the ropes. Eventually, Tony put a down payment on the old building that had been Sloppy Joe's and started to make it a watering hole for the people he took fishing. Tourists started gathering in Key West and bit by bit this place was an attraction again.

So much for the extracurricular activities, back to fishing.

Vance had taken several trips with me, Big Gene, Johnny Potter, and Anthony Saldono, who are all native guides. (Native guides are people born and raised in Key West who fished for a long time.) Vance fell in love with the life style of fishing and boating.

A captain-owner, Dave Patterson, needed a mate. Vance got on board the *Tenacious,* a thirty-eight foot Beckel. It was a brand new boat with a single 671 Detroit engine that goes twenty-five knots. That's fast.

Dave Patterson had been around the charter docks for several years as a photographer, selling eight by ten pictures of the people and their catches. I became acquainted with him then. When he bought his boat and slip on the dock, we became more friendly.

As a new mate, Vance did well. After a few months, Dave had to leave town for a while. I became the captain. We had a father-son team. This was what I wanted with my father but it never happened.

New mates, after a few months, think they know it all, especially if your father is the captain. He would tell me things like, "Dad, go to the West, Johnny caught tuna there yesterday", or "You are going too fast, get out of the weeds, I can't keep the bait clean." I would reply, "I am not your dad on this boat, I'm the captain and everyone does what the captain says or they get off and walk!" So, I decided to hire Big Gene, the fishing machine, to teach Vance. Big Gene is six foot four, two hundred twenty-five pounds. Gene has been fishing in these waters since he was a child. Now he is about thirty-two years of age. The teacher shows Vance several tricks of the trade. How to let the deep troll down fast and smooth, and dropping back to a sailfish with such precision and speed no one know what's happening till he yells "Sail On"!

The father-son team ran the *Tenacious* four or five months. We went out fishing twenty-two to twenty-four days a month, catching fish and sharks. We mounted seven fish in one day when we had a group of Oriental men from San Francisco.

Dave, the owner, decided to get out of the business, so he put the boat up for sale. I would have bought it but the price tag of one hundred-fifty thousand dollars, was too much for me. A guy named Michael Spaulding decided to take it. His nickname became Curly because he shaved his head and had a large-frame build that resembled Curly in the

Three Stooges. Curly and Dave worked out the details, but what about Vance and me?

Chapter 6.
Leasing the Danny III

There was a small Crusader at the opposite end of the dock. It belonged to a guy named Sam Schook from Oregon. He had been fishing in the Keys for a few years. I had several conversations with him about fishing and his home life. He was not happy. Sam went back and forth to Oregon a lot, so the boat sat. The *Danny III* was a thirty-four foot Crusader, equipped with a single 220 Perkins engine, small but adequate and less expensive to run than the *Tenacious*. That was important if I was going to be paying the bills. The mate and I had seen the boat up close and discussed running it together. Vance didn't like it because it was not new and pretty, or was it fast, but it was a job.

Finding someone in Key West is not hard since the island is only two miles wide and four miles long. Sam lived in a condo on the south side along Smathers Beach. I went to see him about running the *Danny III*. Sam, Vance, and I sat down at the kitchen table, drank a beer or two (you can't stand on one leg) and worked out the details. It was a lease plan. I would pay five hundred dollars a month to him and pay all the bills, including dock rent, fuel, bait, etc.

One neat thing Sam said was "I won't put you in business to fail".

I felt confident he would help in any way he could. After a few more beers Vance and I went to the boat and checked it out. The *Danny III* was a solid little boat. The bait was in the freezer, the fuel tank was full, and it had lots of tackle. Vance started making rigs with wire leaders. I checked the engine. We had no money, so getting the first charter was important. The season was on so there were plenty of tourists in town to catch.

Charter boat row has long been a tourist attraction in Key West. In the past, the boats docked along US #1, also called Flagler Boulevard. The state of Florida changed that because of the traffic congestion. People slowed down to look at the catch of fish the charter boats had hanging up. Now, the state built another road that cuts across Garrison Bight. The boats were moved to the other side of the bight. A boat ramp was installed for small boats to launch into the water from their trailers. The City Marina was established and a floating restaurant started business in the sixties. People came to the boats to book charters, see the day's catch, and chat with the captains and mates.

During January, February, and March the weather is unpredictable. That is the time of the year we started this business venture. If the wind blows from the Northeast at less than twenty knots the small boats can fish the south side in the lee of the island, if strong winds come from the east, meaning over fifteen miles per hour, there is nowhere to hide so we stay in port.

Staying in port has its advantages too. There were girls to watch at the Bull, beers to drink at Sloppy's or Captain Tony's. Not being in the party mood, sometimes I'd go to the Houkeelau, a Polynesian restaurant close to the dock. I met a slim, gray haired gentleman in his mid forties who spoke with an English accent. His name was Peter Adair. He was related to the famous oil well fire fighter Red Adair. We got along great. I don't know why, but we did. Peter told me about his friends who had a forty-four foot Nauticat motor sailor. Doc and his captain,

Carol Stob would be coming back from the Bahamas soon.

Someone said the two happiest days in a boat owner's life are the day he buys the boat and the day he sells it. I was thrilled with my little Crusader. I call it little because my dad said, "Don't get on a boat that isn't forty feet long". These thirty-four Crusaders were tough boats and handled well in the bigger seas.

"At last", I thought, "my education from working with other captains will pay off." All the cleaning, painting, and working in dry-dock scraping the bottoms of other people's vessels will help me take care of my boat. When charters get onboard and see a clean, neat, and well maintained fishing boat, as well as the crew, it makes them feel secure, like the crew knows what they are doing.

Owning your own charter boat is a lot of responsibility. The first concern is for the passenger's safety. Then the equipment, such as life jackets, flares, VHF radio, engine, compass, loran, and GPS. How to use the radio! There is more to it than squeezing the mike and talking. It is not a CB radio. No slang is needed. If you have a problem, call the US Coast Guard. A note here: never say "May Day" unless it is a life and death situation. You can say "Pan Pan" if you have an emergency and the Coast Guard will respond on channel sixteen.

When running a charter boat that carries passengers for hire, it is necessary to have a captain's license for six passengers or better. In order to be eligible to take the test for the license, you also need to have at least seven hundred twenty days at sea documented by other captains. It is necessary to be in good health (physical required) as well as having good color vision (color blind test required). The channel markers on the navigation charts as well as the buoys in the water are color coded. They are red, green, white, yellow, and stripped. If the captain can not distinguish between the colors he could get confused on what side of the marker to pass as he goes through a channel or enter a port. I got my license before Vance got to Key West. It takes time and some study from a book called *Chapman Piloting*.

My father, Captain Red, had a master's license that is unlimited and means he could captain any boat or ship to any destination in the world. This is the largest license that is issued.

Chapter 7.
Fun Trip with Vance, Kit, & I on the Miss Gina

Vance and I ran the *Danny III* through the winter and spring. Sometimes when we didn't have a charter, we would take a "fun trip". That's when you get other captains and mates from the dock to go fishing, just for the fun of it. These trips become yelling matches because no one is in charge. Now, isn't that fun?

After the trip is over everyone goes his merry way. Vance and I have to wash the boat and throw away the mounds of beer cans and trash. That's some more fun!

On one of these fun trips, Captain Kit, Vance, and I , went out looking for sailfish. It was in the spring, about the middle of May. The day was perfect. There was light wind, clear sky, and the water was clear and clean with a color change at two hundred feet (a color change is when the water is cobalt blue on the ocean side and aqua blue on the shore side). This happens when the clean water from the deep ocean gets pushed back to the not so clean water from inshore. This is a good place to troll when sailfish are passing through.

Captain Kit was about my age, forty-five, six feet tall, one hundred eighty pounds, silver-gray hair, and Paul Newman eyes.

I drove the boat from the fly bridge. Vance was the mate. Kit held the rod. The first sailfish was hooked. Kit reeled it in quickly, about fifteen minutes. Vance grabbed the bill and released the fish. Next it was my turn. I went down to the deck. Capt. Kit took the wheel. He followed the same course along the color change. We ran four baits. Two of the baits were run out on opposite sides of the boat on the outriggers. Outriggers are long poles mounted on the side of the boat. The lines are attached to the ends of the poles and the poles are extended out from the sides of the boat. The outriggers allow a sport fishing boat to run the fishing lines behind the boat without getting tangled. Two more baits were run from the transom (the transom is the back part of the boat). No deep troll was used. Some captains number the lines

1, 2, 3, 4. I learned to say left rigger, right rigger, left flat line, and right flat line.

A sailfish came up on the left flat line. Kit saw it first, since his vantage point on the fly bridge was much higher.

He yelled, "Sail!"

Vance sprang into action, grabbing the rod and releasing the reel into free spool. This allows the bait to fall naturally and gives the fish time to swallow it whole. Remember, sailfish have no teeth.

Vance yells, "Sail on!"

He handed me the rod. Pull back, wind down, pull back, wind down. I have told charters how to do this hundreds of times. Now it's my time to catch instead of talk.

I say to myself, "that's it, Bud, nice and smooth, no jerks, let the drag do its job". The drag is a clutch in the reel that lets the line out with resistance.

I wind some line in. The fish takes some line out. We go back and forth for fifteen to twenty minutes. It seems a lot longer to me.

Vance said, "It's a nice one, Dad. Do you want to gaff it and mount it?"

I said, "No, let it go. You may catch a bigger one."

Releasing a big fish can be dangerous. The sailfish has a long, pointy bill like a carpenter's rattail file. The bill swings with great force because you are trying to pull him out of the water. With great care, Vance unhooked the line and released the fish.

It is my turn to be the mate, Vance is in the fighting chair, and Kit is at the wheel. I am hot and sweaty. Now is a good time for a beer break. I go get three.

Vance yelled, "Get the line out!"

I replied, "Drink this and shut up!"

I threw Captain Kit a beer on the bridge. Now it is time to relax and reflect. My son and I, with a friend, are fishing off Key West on a beautiful sunshiny day, on my own boat, not paid for, but mine. My dad and Hemingway did this same thing fifty years ago. Two sailfish caught and we have only been out fishing for two hours. I wondered if my dad had this much fun or was it all work and not play?

So much for break time. I put out the left side lines. Vance takes care of the two lines on the other side of the boat. Captain Kit turns the boat around with a wide sweeping motion, so he won't tangle the lines. We cruised back to the same area and depth that we caught the two sailfish. Now all three of us are on edge to see if we can get number three. Catching one was a successful trip, two was great. Three would be fantastic. Time ticks slowly by. All six of our eyes are glued to the baits. A sailfish comes up hot and fast, committing suicide on the left rigger. The line falls, then becomes tight. By the time I get to the rod, the gold Pen International a 50 reel is dumping line fast.

"This is a nice one", I tell Vance.

Vance takes the rod and goes to work. He whips the fish fast, even though the big rascal jumps six or seven times. It was only seven minutes to the boat.

Vance asks "Are we going to mount this one?"

I said, "Yes!"

I grabbed the gaff with my right hand, followed the line down with my left hand. I stuck him behind he head, then he went bizerk. Out of the water he came. I didn't have time to grab hold of the bill which would have given me a little control.

I was trying to hold on and Vance was yelling "Put him in the boat!"

"I am trying!" I yelled back.

The fish takes two or three more jumps before I can grab the bill. Now, into the boat, jam the tail into the corner, and bend the head back to stop him from struggling. Vance slaps him between the eyes with a small bat.

With one last quiver it's over.

Excitement came over all of us at the same time. We had a beer, smoked a cigarette, and expounded on our accomplishments for a while. After our break, I went to the bridge. Vance and Kit cleaned up the boat. Vance retrieved an old army blanket I stowed away for just this occasion. He wrapped the forty-five pound-plus sailfish in the blanket and wet it down while washing the deck. Keeping the fish wet and cool makes the colors last longer.

It was a forty-five minute ride back to the harbor. Vance got the signal flags out to fly on our outriggers. We needed three sailfish pennants.

Flags or pennants are used to notify all within eye sight of a statement or story that needs to be told. In our case, three sailfish were caught. If the flags are upside down the fish were released. In other applications, raising flags could mean sickness aboard the vessel. In that case a solid yellow quarantine flag is raised.

When entering another country such as Cuba or the Bahamas, the proper way to display flags is to fly the flag of the country highest, then the yellow quarantine flag. This means the vessel has just come from outside the country and needs to check in with customs and immigration. Once cleared by the authorities to formally enter the country the quarantine flag is taken down but the country's flag is flown for the duration of the visit.

In days of old there was a need to communicate from vessel to vessel or from ship to land. Many colors and combinations of flags were used to send messages before Marconi invented the telegraph.

Vance called out "Dad, we only have two sailfish flags. What do I do?"
Recalling my experience on other boats I said, "A clean white flag means to repeat, so cut a white cloth to the same size as the pennant and fly it last.'

By this time, we were entering the harbor. We cruised up to the Ocean Key House Hotel. People were standing on the pier, as well as sitting at the dockside bar. My crew held up our catch. Onlookers applauded, took photos, and toasted us with their drinks.

What a great day!

Chapter 8.
Michael Lewis & the Bald Faced Liar Joke

A captain that helped me get started in this business, which I have talked about before, is Michael Lewis. He contributed a lot to my fishing skills as well as helping me put pen to paper now. Michael also wrote fishing articles daily for the Key West Citizen in the early nineties. One of his statements was, "There's only one thing that keeps most fishermen from becoming bald-faced liars."

"What's that?"

"A mustache."

I don't know whether we try to lie or it's a matter of time, but the fish get bigger and the boats get faster.

Chapter 9.
Derrick & the Drunk Front

In the late eighties I was doing well. I had several friends I could count on, my own small charter boat, and half of a duplex I shared with Ed, a guy that had the money for the deposit when the house became available. We had three bedrooms. One for me. One for Ed. The third one we rented out. When the occupant didn't pay the rent then they were fired and they had to go. The house faced the street with all rooms on one floor. It had lots of windows like most southern homes for air ventilation and a cross breeze. On the sides of this place the view was of other buildings but looking out the front the view was open.

At the time of this story the third bedroom

was rented to Derrick and his girlfriend Lovie. He worked for Johnny Potter, the owner of the *Cha Cha*, a charter boat that docked close to my boat. Lovie worked as a waitress at one of the many restaurants in town. She paid the rent every week with one dollar bills. On Friday, when I saw her she would count out one hundred, one dollar bills. Derrick, or as his friends at the dock called him, Shrimp, is five feet six inches tall and two hundred-ten pounds. When he was a young boy he was small and thin That is how he got the nickname Shrimp. Even though he is not small any more, the nickname has stuck. Lovie, his girlfriend never missed a meal either. She was five feet four inches and one hundred-sixty pounds. Both of them had a great sense of humor and laughed a lot.

We would take turns with the cooking and cleaning. All our furniture was used. In the living area we had a chair with a white slip cover (boy was that a mistake), and a couch facing the TV. The dining table and four chairs sat just off the kitchen. Next to the kitchen was a hall to the three bedrooms and single bath. The living room, dining room, and kitchen were all open, like one big room.

Early one morning I was awakened with loud talking and laughing. I got up and walked down the hall in my underwear and T-shirt to the living room to find out what the hell was going on. Shrimp and Lovie were still half drunk from the night before. This was easy to do because the bars inside the city limits didn't close till four in the morning and if every one was ready to party, the airport lounge and the Boca Chica Bar never closed since they were in the county and not required to close.

I yelled, "What the hell time is it and what's all the damn noise about?"

Derrick and Tina, which is Lovie's real name, were kneeling backwards on the couch looking out the windows laughing. As soon as Derrick heard my voice he and Tina got up off the couch and came over to me.

Derrick said, "Come here, you've got to see this."

I said "What Derrick? It's too damn early for this bull shit." He kept insisting I come and look out the window. I did.

Derrick asked, " What do you see?"

I said, "A big black cloud. It's going to rain and we don't have to go to the boat today."

He replied, " No Bud, It's a drunk front. We have to get drunk today."

I said, "We have to?"

Derrick demanded, "Yes, we have to!"

So, even though it was only seven thirty in the morning I washed my face, combed my hair, and got dressed. The three of us drove my little baby shit yellow AMC station wagon to the liquor store to get a quart of vodka, a quart of orange juice, and ice.

In the late eighties no one ever thought about drinking and driving. It was a way of life for the crowd I ran around with. Most of them were my son's age, twenty years younger than me. I was not a very good influence for these young people but I was in my early forties and just had my second divorce and I wanted to be free to do what ever came up and so I did.

After loading up on libations we proceeded on one of our Conch tours. We drove around the island past the beach to see if any girls were out in their bathing suits and then down the boulevard past the charter boats to check if any of them were sinking. We paid the most attention to my boat and Derrick's. If a mate like Derrick or any of the good mates works on a boat they call it their boat. After we checked the bulges to make sure there was no water accumulation, we went down to the Schooner Wharf.

On these rainy days most of the carpenters, fishermen, and tourists gather at the watering all over town, so you have to stop at each one. This means two drinks at the Schooner Wharf, two drinks at the Bull, and we can't forget Rick's, and Sloppy Joe's, two drinks each, plus we have our cups full between bars. By three o'clock it's time to go home and take a nap.

"Good Night"

Chapter 10.
Carol & Bud Meet & Purchase the Miss Gina

Peter Adair, a man I had met and had drinks with several times in the last months, called me early one morning. I said early, which to me meant nine or ten on the days I didn't have a fishing trip. Peter spoke with an English accent. He was born in Rhodesia, now Zimbabwe, and was educated in England. His salt and pepper, short, clean and neat hair gave him a distinguished look. He had a medium build, about five feet-ten and one hundred-fifty pounds. He always dressed well.

Peter retired after he invented the porcelain cap for dentures in conjunction with Dow Corning. Now he lived in Key West and painted landscapes in water colors.

Peter told me his friend with the sailboat would be coming back from the Bahamas this afternoon. We would be meeting them at the Houkeelou Bar for cocktails at 3 P.M.

I got there on time. Peter was already on his second drink. Peter told me who was coming. Doctor Mori, a prosthetic surgeon from Boston who owned the boat, Carol Stob, the boat's captain, and a few more of Doc's friends. After Peter and I ordered another round, a group of people came up to Peter. There was the usual hugging, shaking of hands, and introductions. Carol asked if she could sit on the empty seat next to me.

I said "Of course'.

She sat down, ordered a vodka and diet coke, and then told me she had heard from Peter about a Conch fisherman and she was interested in learning how to fish. She had a captain's license and took care of Doc's boat, as well as living aboard at Oceanside Marina on Stock Island, the next island up from Key West towards Miami. I told Carol I would be happy to show her about sport fishing. We could have a free fun trip. A few days later, we gathered at my boat about eight in the morning. Carol brought beer and sandwiches. I had the boat, bait, and rods ready. Carol learned how to bait a hook, let the deep troll ball down, and techniques for finding fish. She was amazed as we went into shallow water (about four feet deep), that sport fishing boats, unlike sailboats that need to stay in six to eight feet of water, did not go aground. Doc learned some things too. He was not the owner or master of my boat. I yelled at him to "leave the rods alone and sit down!" Everyone looked at me like I had just slapped the Pope.

After that day, Carol and I spent a lot of time together eating out and meeting in the afternoon at the dock.

One day, Carol and I were at the *Danny III* catching up on repairs, when the phone rang. It was Sam, the man whom I leased the *Danny III* from.

Sam said he needed money. "Could I buy the boat?"

I said, "I didn't have any money when I started this venture, and I don't have much more now."

I called to Carol "Sam wants to sell the boat."

She asked "How much?"

Sam gave me a price of $35,000.

Carol replied "Will he take $10,000 down and the rest in monthly payments?"

Sam agreed. He would be in Key West in a few days to fill our the paper work and transfer the title. Carol agreed to provide the $10,000 down, and I would make the easy monthly payments, just like I had been making under the lease agreement. Carol wanted to know what interest rate I would pay her for the $10,000 loan. I told her she would get to take all the trips on the boat she wanted, plus take part in the fun trips with the guys.

Carol and I wrote an agreement on the monthly payments and length of the payout. We also specified the lease with the city of Key West, on the dock space at the City Marina, as well as all the equipment aboard the boat and the freezers, phones, and items on the dock that were included in the sale. Sam came to town a few days later. He agreed with the plan and we changed the documentation into my name. Vessels have the option of being documented with the federal government as well as registered in the state they are docked. As well as the paper change, I changed the name of the boat from *Danny III* to *Miss Gina.*

When changing a name on a boat there are a lot of considerations, such as karma. Traditionally, fishing boats are named after women, so do you put your wife's name on the transom or maybe your girl friend's?

I said to myself, "wife's and girl friends come and go, but your daughter will always be your daughter." Gina, my daughter, was in college and not married, hence the name, *Miss Gina.*

Chapter 11.
Lady With the Tube Top on Miss Gina

I remember this trip well because it's the only trip I thought I might have over stepped my bounds as a boat captain and as a male.

It was the early part of June. The first two weeks are the best time to fish for dolphin and the worst time for vacationing people. The winter tourists have all gone home and school is not out so the summer people are not in Key West yet.

Vance and I were sitting at our place behind the *Miss Gina* drinking a cold beer. We were hot and sweaty. There were a few clouds in the sky to give a little shade. We normally stay at the dock until five o'clock or till we book a charter. This afternoon two people drove up behind the boat. They got out of their car and walked up and asked if we were open for charter tomorrow. I said, "Yes." Vance got our picture book out and showed the people pictures of the kind of fish we catch this time of year.

The couple was from Alexandria, Virginia. They had a second home on Big Pine Key which is twenty miles north of Key West. I guessed their age to be mid forties. Their dress was casual but not cheap. I notice clothes, rings, watches, and cars when people approach the boat to tell if the people can afford the trip. No need to spend a lot of time talking to someone who can't afford the trip and miss talking to a real prospective charter. The man was big, six feet, two hundred-thirty pounds. The lady was five feet six inches tall, one hundred-forty pounds. If we happen to hang into a large marlin that is two hundred pounds plus it is an asset to have charters that are big and healthy enough to catch the fish.

After talking a while and sharing a beer, which I keep plenty of in the freezer for just this type of occasion, they gave us a deposit for tomorrow's charter. They told us he was in the carpet business and she was in real estate. They might have some guests along tomorrow. I said we can take up to six people. I also explained they should bring their own food and drinks. They wanted to know what kind of beer we drank and what sort of sandwiches we liked. Vance told them Budweiser was good for the beer, ham or roast beef was great for the sandwiches. I agreed.

The next morning Vance showed up at seven thirty to do his job as a mate, check the engine oil and water, and get ice out of the freezer. We make our own ice in five gallon plastic buckets. We use some for the fish we will catch. The ice on the fish keeps them from spoiling in the hot sun even though we have four long insulated igloo coolers. Vance also gets the bait out of the freezer. For an eight hour, full-day trip we take six bags of bait. Three bags of larger bait are packed with 12 ballyhoo to a bag. Three bags of smaller bait are packed 20 to a bag.

The couple show up along with another couple about the same age. Shortly after everyone was aboard and all the gear was stowed, we head out or as they say in nautical terms we were under way making way. This day started out like hundreds of other trips I had taken. Vance put the outriggers down so they would not hit the two bridges. We idled past the Coast Guard housing, through the bridges, and into the harbor where he put the rigger's up after the second bridge.

Vance always did well explaining what was going to happen and how to handle the big fifty pound test rods and reels. This time of year there was no stopping the boat until we reached six hundred feet of water. This takes an hour or more heading due south out of the harbor. While we are cruising out, I always look towards the sky for birds such as small terns circling and diving or the big black frigate bird with his six foot wing span gliding on the heat currents in the light blue sky. Frigate birds have great eye sight. They can see large fish from several hundred feet above the water and they follow the fish around while the fish are looking for small bait fish to eat, so if anyone on the boat sees a frigate I steer the boat in the bird's direction.

This day no birds were seen so we settled for a sea weed line. These lines run east and west and are loaded with bait fish, sticks, large boards and all sorts of trash. The dolphin like to cruise along these weed lines to eat as well as for the shade.

We headed east because I saw other boats already heading west and I would be the only one going east.

Vance put out lines and lowered the deep troll to forty feet. Now we wait. After an hour or so we had caught a few dolphin, ten to fifteen pounds each. I called Vance up to the bridge to take the wheel so he could take a break and cool down and I went down to the cockpit to play the mate and chat with the people. They were more my age than Vance's. I like to see how many fish they want to take home or if they are looking to mount a big dolphin. The usual questions were asked. How long had I been a charter captain? Is this my boat? I answer their questions and they answer mine. I ate my sandwich and we settle down to wait for the next strike. After a while of rolling up and down and back and forth Vance yells, "Right rigger!"

I look in that direction. I could see a big bull dolphin speeding with his head making a wake towards the right rigger bait. I leaped towards the rod to be ready if he grabbed the bait. It's hard to watch the fish and do nothing but if everything is just right the big bull will not pass it by.

The lady that chartered the boat was standing next to me. I told her to sit down. She did. She was wearing sandals, shorts and a green tube top. The fish grabbed the ballyhoo and took off away from the boat. The line snapped off the rigger clip. I grabbed the rod. The line was streaming out of the reel at a great rate of speed. Some fish can swim up to fifty or sixty miles per hour. I tried to put the rod in the gimble between her legs. This is hard to do on most women because they are told all their lives to keep their knees together or cross their legs, but after I yelled, "Spread your legs" for the second time ,she complied. I instructed her on how to hold the rod and how to pull the rod back then lower the rod and wind the handle on the reel as it goes down.

Now I have to get the deep troll up and out of the way so the line doesn't get cut, reel in the other lines so they won't get tangled. This only takes a few minutes. All this time I tell the other people to take a seat or go up to the fly bridge. Just get out of the way because we have a big fish on the line and we need to catch it. By this time the big boy is beginning to tire. I can tell by the way the reel is slowing down. Also it seems my angler is beginning to tire. I notice that every time she lowers the rod she stops instead of pulling up right away. Then I saw what she was doing. She would pull up her tube top with her right thumb and forefinger instead of pulling the rod back with both hands. This pause could cost us this fish if it charged the boat or jumped out of the water. The slack in the line would allow the hook to be thrown out of the fishes mouth by the shaking of it's head.

My response was to yell loudly, "Stop pulling up your top. We have all seen tits before but we haven't seen that fish in this boat!"

I got a strong look from the lady but she stopped pulling her top up for the rest of the fight, which was not over yet. Big bull dolphin will jump if they're hooked in the mouth but if they are hooked deep in the stomach they generally don't jump. This fish took a few jumps and we got a good look at him. It was a beauty. Thirty-five pounds plus. I can tell the weight or get close because I see and feel hundreds of them each year.

Even though the fight between the lady with the tube top and the big bull dolphin had only been going on for fifteen minutes she was tired and sweating. Her fore arms and fingers on her left hand were starting to cramp. This comes from squeezing the rod too tight. It's necessary to hold the rod tight but only tight enough to keep control. She began to complain about the heat and pain.

I asked her if she would like to give up the rod. I said, "I could get a man to bring this fish in."

She responded, "Hell no, I'll get the son of a bitch in if it kills me!"

A few minutes later the big one was whipped. He came slowly up to the boat and I stuck him with the gaff, and dragged it into the fish box. Even though a large fish is in the box the fight still goes on for a while. Sometimes the fish flops it's tail hard enough to kick open the top. If this happens, it is possible for him to flip and flop out of the box back into the water. I sat on the top of the fish box so this would not happen. I was facing the lady angler. I apologized for my gruffness and explained I felt I had to make her mad so she would continue the fight with aggression and she did and the fish was in the box. The lady put the rod back in the rod holder on the side of the boat while still seated. Then she turned to look at me with her hair a mess and some strands in her eyes and said, "I don't think I could have done it if you hadn't made me mad. Let's have a beer."

    I try to finish a trip on a good note and this was it so we turned the boat for home port.

Chapter 12.
Victor is Hired & the Sick Boy Catches a Sailfish

The best way to get charters in those days was to sit on the dock behind your boat. There was an unwritten agreement among all of the thirty to thirty-five captains at the City Marina that you don't talk to a potential charter until he was on the dock behind your boat. The dock had to be attended by the captain or the mate from seven in the morning till seven in the evening, unless you were fishing, to talk to the people that drive by to ask questions about the price or availability of fishing. Around four in the afternoon, the boats start coming back from their full-day trips. After the vessel is docked, the mate wets down the hot concrete dock so he can unload the fish. He rinses off the fish and hangs them up so the charters can take photographs of their catch. This is the prime time of the day to get the next day's charter.

After a few days of sitting on the dock, unable to get a charter, Vance decides it's the boat's fault. The boat is too small for him. He goes three docks over to work on the *Cha Cha*. The owner, Captain Johnny Potter, is a young man about the same age as Vance. The *Cha Cha* is a forty-five foot, #1 hull, built in Key West by Conchs. With its sixteen foot beam, generator, air conditioning, and new appearance, it makes it much easier to book a charter.

A mate in training that had some experience, came to see me. He said he heard I needed a mate and he needed a job. His name was Victor. This man was forty-five years old, small framed and weighed about one hundred fifty-five pounds. He was five feet five inches tall, with wiry red hair pulled back into a short pony tail. His white skin was freckled and wrinkled from the sun.

I was sitting in the shade of my umbrella drinking a cold one. I asked Victor if he would like a beer.

He said, "Sure, the sun is over the yardarm somewhere." This is an old sailor's expression meaning that the sun is setting and it is lower than the yard or support that holds the sail.

The City Marina is located on the body of water called Garrison Bight. The *Miss Gina* was the first boat the cars passed after they drove under the Garrison Bight bridge. Amenities are few as marinas go: a dockmaster's office (the dockmaster is the person in charge of all activities and problems that take place in the marina), a floating restaurant, shower, and toilet. They have about fifty slips for transient boats. On the dock behind the *Miss Gina* were two large wooden cabinets twelve feet by four feet by four feet. Inside one cabinet, we had a large freezer for bait. The other cabinet had the phone, tools, and maintenance parts. These cabinets are called dock boxes. A little aside: someone once described a women to me as "dumb as a dock box."

Victor and I made a plan on how to split up the time sitting at the dock booking the boat. He would take the morning shift (7 till 1). I would be there from noon till five. We also discussed wages. I told him I would pay forty dollars for a half day and fifty dollars for a full day. He would get one third of the money for a fish mount, one third of the money for fish sold to the market, and keep all of his tips. I also told him I would guarantee him fifty dollars for half day and one hundred dollars for a full day trip if the customers did not give him that much or there were no mounts or fish sale money. There were very few trips when it was necessary for me to add to his pay. Fish money depends on the price at the market and how many fish the charters want us to fillet for them, so they can take the fish home. The mounts depend on the mate. He has to help the charters catch the fish and then talk the angler into putting it on the wall.

Victor and I worked well together. During the first weeks, we caught some fish, sold some fish, and mounted some fish with Phluger Taxidermy in Ft. Lauderdale.

Now it was March, a dreaded month, because the wind blew fifteen to twenty-five knots almost every day. The wind and fishing conditions are closely related. The size of the boat also makes a difference in the comfort of the passengers. My barometer for the wind in my thirty-four foot crusader was up to ten knots of wind was great. Ten to fifteen knots was bumpy. Over fifteen knots the waves got white caps on them and the unaware and unskilled person would stumble and could fall due to the shifting of the boat from side to side and up and down. My dad told me not to get on any boat under forty feet, but the thirty-four crusader I called *Miss Gina*, was all I could afford now and with its single engine it was cheap to operate.

Fishing is affected by the wind blowing as well. The more the wind howls the more sand is kicked up off the bottom causing the water to be murky or milk like. The fish can't see the bait swimming on the top as I troll by. If they can't see the bait they can't bite it.

When I got to the dock one afternoon, Victor had spoken to a father and son. They left a one hundred dollar deposit for the next day, if the wind was calm enough.

The father said, "Son has been very sick and he needs smooth water."

I arrived the next morning at eight with my sandwich and drink in a brown sack. Victor and the charter were there and ready. The father and son talked a lot about sailfish and how the boy would like to mount one. I said that catching a sailfish was physically taxing. Since the boy had been sick, maybe we should concentrate on other species of fish. No dice.

The boy was in his mid twenties, five feet eight inches tall and weighed one-hundred, twenty pounds. I was on the bridge thinking to myself, "I have a new mate that's never caught a sailfish, or boated one, and I have a young man who just got out of the hospital with some kind of a liver disease. Well, I can only control the boat, not the weather, not the fish, and the weather looks good."

Heading one hundred eighty degrees due south, to the sea buoy, the water looked good. Not too clear, but enough for what we were looking for, the pointy nosed, elusive sailfish. I slowed the engine down to trolling speed. The mate let out the rigger lines one hundred feet behind the boat. He put the flat line twenty feet back. Victor asked how deep he should put the deep troll.

I said, "Twenty-five feet."

Sometimes you can use a deep troll, sometimes not, although I have caught sails on the deep troll. We started to troll in one hundred feet deep water at the sea buoy, still heading south.

A few minutes passed.

Victor yells, "Sail on!"

The fish was on the right rigger. The line snapped loose. As it fell, the mate grabbed the rod and released the reel into free spool.

The line became tight causing the reel to scream. Victor locked down the drag. The fifty pound rod was bent into a "C" shape.

Victor yells, "Sail on!"

At the same time, I saw the fish jump out of the water. A good one, it should weigh at least thirty pounds. This one looked big enough to kill and mount, if only the angler can handle the rod.

I yelled, "Son, get into the fighting chair!"

Victor keeps the line tight so the fish can't throw the hook, and walks the rod to the boy in the fighting chair. Next, Victor brings all the other lines into the boat. The fight is on.

I helped the boy by backing up the boat at a slow pace. It made retrieving the two hundred yards of line the fish has taken off the spool easier.

The young man turned the handle for five minutes or so and then stopped.

I yelled, "Tell him to turn the handle!"

Victor replied, "Bud, he is throwing up."

"When he is done, tell him to turn the handle!" I said.

After that momentary pause, the son went back to work, with me backing down and him winding in. Victor got the gaff. He started walking to the right side of the cockpit and I said, "No, go to the left side. You are right handed, gaff on your right, grab the bill with your left hand".

Now it's crunch time. The angler needs to stay in the chair. The mate needs to gaff the fish and at the same time pull up and grab the bill and not get stabbed. One last splash and Victor lifted him into the boat.

I yelled, "Jam him into the corner and bend his head back!"

To which Victor replied, "I will, just as soon as he gets his fin off my neck".

After a few minutes, I checked my watch. One hour, fifteen minutes from the time we cast off the dock lines till the fish was in the boat. That must be some kind of a record. At least it was my personal best. I came down from the bridge to congratulate the man.

I saw him on the couch, not looking well. I asked if he heeded to go back to the dock or would he be able to stay out.

He sat up, looked me in the eye, and said, "Now I want dad to catch one."

Victor, standing next to me, tried to explain that people come to the keys for thirty years in hopes of catching one sailfish, much less two in one day. The father chimed in that is was up to the boy. If he felt up to it, he would try.

So, back to work. Victor put the lines out. I was at the helm. We cruised around the area for a little while. Another strike! Another sailfish jumped in the background!

Now it's dad's turn in the fighting chair. Victor gave him the rod. Victor retrieved the other lines.

The angler's line went slack, and dad stopped winding.

"Well, I guess he got away!" He said.

I yelled, "Wind! Wind! He is coming towards the boat!"

I moved the boat to tighten the line and there still was no fish. Gone, the losing of fish is as much a part of fishing as the catching. All we needed was one fish, and God must have wanted that young man to catch it.

By this time in my career, I have been a fisherman for five or six years. I've never heard of nor had I caught a sailfish in one hour fifteen minutes from start to finish.

We called it a half-day and went back to the dock to sign the papers for mounting this sailfish. It cost about one hundred dollars per foot to reproduce, ship, and pay commission on most mounts.

Chapter 13.
Blondel Hancock, Commercial Fishing

In my father's younger days, people of the Keys were poor, but out there, there were few, if any, laws pertaining to fishing. Common sense was the law. Take a little, leave a little, then we can fish this spot again tomorrow. Now, it's let's kill them all and let Leo sort them out (Leo is the local fish wholesaler or fishmonger, as they used to be called). I saw great changes in the time I spent as a charter boatman, such as saltwater fishing license, saltwater product license, restricted species license, limits for king mackerel (four per person to two per person), and the size of the fish (eighteen inches, then seventeen inches). Every few months there was a new law. At the dock, the rules changed as well, like buying your boat slip from another person that is leaving or quitting the business, city and county occupational license, water, electric, and insurance bills, and then the city of Key West telling us how much liability insurance we must carry. The last count was a minimum of one million dollars.

I had a friend who fished commercially for a living most of his life. His name was Blondel Hancock. At the time I met him, he was running a thirty-four foot Crusader powered by a single 453 cubic-inch Detroit Diesel. This was a good economical engine and seaworthy boat. The boats name was the *Cha Cha*. Yes, the same as Johnny Potter's sport fishing charter boat. It's OK and legal to have boats of the same name.

Blondel had a brother, Manual, who also fished. Manual Hancock was a young man in the early forty's, who took over running my father's boat, the *Evelyn*, when Red went into the Coast Guard. Manual told me it was the happiest day of his life when he became the captain of the *Evelyn*. He got the job because he used to hang out at the boat a lot with Red and was there when Red was conscripted.

The only redeeming factor about commercial fishing for yellowtail snapper is the people who do it, love it. You are on your own, no one telling you what to do or how to do it. Some boats carry their families on these three or more day trips. Some take one or two people.

Blondel fished mostly alone. When he had other people they made messes or mistakes that he had to clean up or straighten out. The *Cha Cha* was kept at the fish house where they got fuel and sold the fish. The dockage was free. He ran the boat on three-day trips. The *Cha Cha* carried a small skiff, twelve hundred pounds of ice, food such as eggs, flour, beans, lots of Cuban coffee, and fish.

Blondel would leave the dock at first light. Loaded, he would cruise west, to one of several islands that were dotted from Key West to the Tail End Bowie. The Tail End Bowie is the last navigational buoy heading west. After picking a spot to anchor the *Cha Cha*, he launched the little skiff. With the cast net in the skiff, he would row over to shallow water looking for birds diving and feeding. Blondel handled the skiff with one oar out the stern, undulating back and forth pushing the skiff forward. When he got to the right spot, he would cast the net and retrieve mahoa or pilchers (pilchers are larger than mahoa-half inch wide and one and a half inch long) to be used as bait for the day and night of catching yellow tails. This is not fishing, this is catching. No fish, no pay.

When he had caught enough bait, he rowed back to the *Cha Cha*, secured the skiff, raised the anchor, and cruised to a spot in the waters from forty to one hundred twenty-five feet deep, anchored the *Cha Cha*, and started a chum slick with the freshly caught bait. (A chum slick is chopped small bits and pieces of fish that are thrown overboard behind the boat creating an oily glaze on the water surface.) After a few hours, the water gets a yellow haze. The yellowtail snappers are there.

The yellowtail snapper feed not on the top or the bottom, they feed in the middle so the chum from the boat slowly drifts back and down into the water twenty-five to fifty feet behind the boat gathering in a large school of fish.

To catch them, he used a hand line, not a rod and reel, because there was nothing to break and they were faster. He put small bicycle inner tube rubber on his index finger so as not to cut the finger as the fish takes off. Some of the fish grow to four or five pounds and put up a good fight. Upon hooking up, the line was retrieved with a hand-over-hand motion, then into the dehooker. (Dehooker-a box with a heavy wire bend into the shape of a large M.) Keeping the hook tight against the wire, the fish wiggled until it came off and fell into the chill barrel (chill barrel-sea water and ice which was extremely cold), which killed the fish quick, not letting it jump and thrash about. Then Blondel would use his forefinger and thumb holding the hook, made two short stabs at the bait, putting two mahoa on the hook, and then out in the water again. This whole procedure only took one to one and a half minutes. This went on until the fish stopped biting, which might be one or two hours. He gutted the fish he had caught, packed them in ice, and waited until night to start again, and so on until six hundred pounds or more were caught. When the ice got low it was time to go home, sell the fish, and sleep in his bed at home for a few nights.

When a commercial fisherman went fishing, he checked the price per pound before going, because it had to be high enough to cover the cost and give him a profit. He could only carry a limited amount of fish back to sell because of the amount of ice he carried and time it would last. A lot of times, if the weather had been pretty calm, newcomers to the Keys, (the people that sold their houses and businesses in the north) would get a boat, a saltwater product license, go fishing, and sell their fish to pay for their expenses. This kind of action by forty or fifty newcomers, who have nothing to do because they sold their two-hundred-thousand dollar houses and had retirement incomes, could drop the price of fish form three dollars-sixty cents a pound to two dollars-forty cents a pound in one day. For the commercial fisherman like Blondel, by the time they get back to the fish house from a three-day trip, this price drop made the difference between a profitable trip and a loss. This never did seem right to me. Men trying to make a living in the place they were born, at a trade their fathers taught them, are suffering because of some others who don't have anything else to do. I think it is OK to go catch fish. Give them to their friends and neighbors, but don't sell them to the market and knock the price down for the people that do this for a living.

Chapter 14.
Naked Charter on Miss Gina with Kit & Victor

Running your own boat means making the decisions about all sorts of things, such as, when to pull the vessel out of the water to clean and paint the bottom, polish the chrome, and varnish the bright work (bright work is the wood that needs to be varnished). I tried to fix, or maintain, one piece of equipment every day. I saved the most intensive labor for the fall when the charters are few. Victor and I were polishing the chrome on just such a day. Of course, when doing such intense labor, one needed to take rest and drink a beer every now and then. We were sitting on the bench, facing towards the stern of the boat, discussing what should be the next task. A late-model Chevy pulled up in one of the two parking places behind my boat. A man and woman got out of the car and asked if we were open tomorrow.

I said, "Yes, did he want to charter the whole boat or a split charter?" (A split charter was two couples shared in the full price-each couple pay half.)

He explained he had two other women beside his wife that would be going. I told him a full day for his party would be five hundred dollars and we needed a one hundred dollar deposit. We would leave at eight in the morning. He should bring the food and drinks for his party. The man told me he should get a discount because the girls wanted to get naked and we would get a kick out of that. I explained the cost of running the boat didn't change because of the circumstances. The price was five hundred dollars with a one hundred dollar deposit. He then handed me a Visa card for the deposit.

As they drove away, Victor and I had another Budweiser and discussed the ramifications of this charter. What to do, since he was not married or had a girl friend-no problem there. As for me, I could get into deep trouble with Carol by having too much fun. I called my old friend, Captain Kit, to see if he would take the trip. Kit wasn't married nor did he have any serious relationship going on at the time, so no one to answer to about what happened on the trip if word got out about the naked group. On the other hand, I was living with Carol and didn't want to cause her any embarrassment so Kit was the man for this job. Stevie Wonder could see that.

He said, "Yes, it sounds like a fun thing to do".

When the charter was over, Kit and Victor told me about the day. It seems that as they were trolling the two women stayed on the bridge with Kit and took off all their clothes, down to their birthday suits. The man and his wife also got totally naked in the cockpit with Victor. Captain Kit told the other fishing boats what was happening by way of the VHF radio. Before long there were eight or ten boats circling the little *Miss Gina*, all getting a good look at the girls waving.

The next day, Carol captained the half-day charter with Victor. While trolling along the reef, she got a call on the VHF radio, "*Miss Gina, Miss Gina.*"

Carol picked up the microphone and answered, "*Miss Gina* here".

The radio was dead calm for a few minutes, then a man's voice said, "O, I thought Bud was captaining the boat today."

She replied, "No, he had something else to do today".

The voice said, "I was wondering about yesterday's charter".

She said, "I know all about it and I am glad everyone had a great time".

Chapter 15.
Art Cole & The Six Sailfish Day

Key West in the eighties' and nineties' was a lot of fun. Maybe it was my age, or just at the right time and place. Fishing was great most every day, except when the wind howled which made the trips miserable and wet.

In the spring, April, May, and June, the sailfish came. One of my trips, I had two young men for a charter. The mate was Art Cole. We headed to Sand Key Light to start. (Sand Key Light is seven miles south of Key West. It is one of several lights erected in the 1880's by the US Coast Guard along the Keys so the commercial ships would not run aground on the reef.)

Art put out four lines, no feathers and no deep troll. Two of the lines were placed close to the boat and two rigger lines long, about one hundred feet back. We ran a rubber squid teaser to make splashes in front of the flat line. If fish attack the teaser, the flat line bait can be pulled forward at a swift retrieve and attract the fish to the bait. If the fish notices the bait, it is free spooled to let it fall as if it had been hit. The boat never changed speed until the angler had received the rod with the sailfish hooked up.

This day we had six strikes by sailfish, each of the two men had caught a sailfish and four other fish jumped off. Upon returning to the dock, the customers got off my boat and went down the dock to see what the other boats had caught. They did not understand what a great day we had. Catching a sailfish is rare. They only pass Key West in the spring and fall for a short time each season as they travel in search of food. I have fished people that would have given a lot of money to catch just one.

Chapter 16.
Funeral at Sea

My first funeral at sea was for a friend of Anthony and Johnny's. He had been cremated the day before. We were to sprinkle the ashes at sea. I donated my boat and a day's pay so they could take several boats and socialize with the rest of the mourners.

Vance and I made the boat ready that Sunday morning before anyone arrived. It was in the fall, October or November. The wind was still out of the south, like in the summer. The day was clear and the sun was starting to warm and dry up the morning dew.

I sat in my captain's chair waiting for the guests like all the other charter boats except this was going to be a sad occasion. I didn't know exactly what to expect or what to do at one of these funerals such as where to go or how deep should the water be.

I had been baptized twenty years before in West Texas as a Baptist. I had been to several land based funerals. I knew from my experience as well as from talking to my friends, Captain Curly Spaulding, there are many different types of funeral services. Curly had been a mortician in Detroit before he came to Key West. He spoke of several different traditional ways of burial. In a Jewish funeral the casket is lowered into the earth, the dirt is shoveled on the top as the final words are spoken. The Baptists lower the casket last, after the ceremony. Some people are buried in a mausoleum, others are cremated and the ashes sprinkled out of planes or off rock ledges at the edge of the ocean or river.

Anthony showed up first, then Johnny. Vance and Johnny made sure there was enough ice for beer and bait.

I asked, "Why do we need bait?"

Johnny replied, "You never leave the dock without beer and bait!"

The people started showing up in ones and twos. Soon we had a nice group of fifteen to eighteen people. Some of them I knew, most I had never seen before. Even though Key West is a small island, the people gather in different cliques socially.

Anthony suggested we take the boats out to the gulf because the wind was out of the southeast. This would make the seas calmer behind the island. I yelled to Vance to cast off the lines and we were underway to a burial at sea. After leaving the marina area I called Anthony to ask exactly where we were going.

He said, "Go out the Calda Channel."

I told him, "I have never taken the Calda Channel."

Johnny was listening to the radio as well. They got a big laugh that I had never taken this shortcut and indicated I should follow them closely.

The Calda Channel is seldom used by large boats because is snakes and twists in very shallow water. The channel shoals up from time to time because of the changing sands after a storm. It is best for larger boats to go through there at high tide. Being unfamiliar with this channel, I followed their boats closely.

We arrived at the burial spot in the Gulf of Mexico about forty-five minutes after we left the dock. The eulogy was spoken, the ashes were poured from the urn, and fresh flowers were thrown into the water. It was a simple, beautiful service.

Chapter 17.
Derelict Boat Towing

Before I got the *Ms. Gina*, I met two guys that had a contract from the city and county to remove the derelict vessels. Bobby Andraseckes and Gino Robison came to me at the charter boat dock in an eighteen foot runabout with an outboard engine. They tied up to the *Miss Gina* and asked if I wanted a beer.

"But, of course!" I said.

They proceeded to tell me their problem. After spending weeks gathering old sunken boats and pieces of old boats, they needed to move them out past the reef to a designated spot located by the Coast Guard and the Florida Marine Patrol.

It was summer. The weather was hot and sultry. The charters were few. So, I listened to them, and we consumed a lot of beer. They told me what had been found on one of the vessels. They found a duffel bag that contained human bones and a chain. According to the police, this person had been missing for a long time. A forensic specialist using the dental records had identified the body.

At the end of this long conversation, we agreed on a price for the *Miss Gina* to tow these derelict vessels, which was less than a full-day's charter. Carol and I, on the *Miss Gina*, would meet them the next morning at a place on the east side between Key West and Stock Island.

The water was shallow there, but the bottom was mostly sand and we had a keel to protect the hull. Bobby had connected a long towline from this large pile of floating junk. I backed up to it and Carol made a towing bridle, and then tied the line to it. The bridle on our stern would allow the towline to slide back and forth from port to starboard. Bobby and Gino wore radio headphones for communication. Gino was in the skiff, Bobby on board the *Miss Gina* with Carol and I.

Off we go, pulling this mass of hulls stacked on top of, and shoved into each other. I start slow, tightening the line so as to check out the security of the lines as well as the stability of the tow. We must keep everyone away from the lines, especially at the start, because if the main line breaks under stress, it would pop like a whip and hurt someone.

Everything is fine, so off to our destination we go. It's seven miles to the reef, then another mile or two to the spot where we are to sink this stuff to make an artificial reef. An orange poliball had been set at the designated spot, in about one hundred-ninety feet of water. This is deep enough not to be a hazard to any ship or sailing vessel.

The tow is back one hundred feet and had no steerage, so it whips slowly from side to side causing *Miss Gina*'s stern to lean from side to side. It was that time of the year when the lobster traps had just been set. There were thousands of eight inch Styrofoam balls floating every twenty or thirty feet in all directions in the shallow strip between Key West and the reef. Each of the traps was twenty-four inches wide, twenty-four inches tall, and thirty-six inches long, made of wood containing seventy-five pounds of concrete in the bottom to keep them in place when the current and tide flow. Trying to navigate the vessel in a straight course and dodging the trap lines was next to impossible. If I snagged one, Bobby would tell Gino on the radio headset and Gino would maneuver the skiff with a small outboard to the line and cut it free. If I gathered too many of these traps, the combined weight of them might stop me from making way. (Making way means moving forward.) Traveling at five knots, fight current, traps, and the lateral movement of the tow, it took two and a half hours to make the trip. I took the helm first, then Carol. Bobby said I hit all the traps and Carol missed or maneuvered around the ones that were in front of her.

Crossing the reef at last, we could see the poliball and the Marine Patrol boat in the distance. The current was ripping to the west at five knots or so (a knot is almost a mile per hour). We were east of the site. I had to get to the spot, and then turn around so the boat could hold the salvage in place against the current. Gino came and picked up Bobby. They went to the tow. Bobby boarded and went below to light the dynamite he had previously placed inside the soon-to-be reef. He placed a large metal tank on top of the charge to hold it in place. Bobby and Gino returned to my vessel. Bobby explained that after the charge went off, the tow would slowly sink and I should hold it in place until he said to cut the line. A few minutes later, BOOM! Some dust and debris flew into the sky. The heavy metal heat exchanger shot fifty to eighty feet straight up, then with a nice curve returned to the sea and sank to the bottom.

As the tow filled with water, it got heavier and heavier. It started to go down. The current was pushing against us. I gave more and more throttle. We were still moving backwards, not staying in place or moving ahead. Five minutes passed. You could only see half of the sinking salvage. The towline was so tight, a tight rope walker could practice his trade on it.

I yelled to Bobby, "Can I cut the line now?"

He said, "Not yet."

"Bobby, I'm going backward fast!"

With the weight of the wreck full of water, and the current moving in the same direction, the stress on the little thirty-four Crusader and the single Perkins engine was being pulled backwards as well as down into the water.

I called again to Bobby and said, "I am going to cut the tow line!"

He said, "OK, Now!"

It only took two cuts on the one-inch line to relieve the pressure, and the derelict vessels became an artificial reef.

It was our job to remove any and all of the floating debris. Amazingly, less than a dozen small boards were left.

After sinking and all was clear, the Marine Patrol Officer came over to us and said, "This was the closest sinking he had ever experienced." We had sunk the vessels directly on the spot where the officials had designated.

Carol took the wheel, Gino tied off his skiff to the stern of *Miss Gina*, and we all had several beers for a job well done.

Chaprter 18.
Carol's Dad Dies, Feb., '91

A few weeks before the trip with Johnny and Anthony, Carol Stob, my significant other, had to leave Key West to take care of her aging father. She had just bought a new Jeep Wrangler when word got to us that her father wasn't doing well. She packed her things and headed to South Padre Island, Texas. This kind of breaking up of a relationship came hard for both of us, not knowing what might happen in the future.

I got a call from Carol three weeks later, saying her dad had died and could I come to South Padre Island and help her, since she had no living relatives. I said yes and made arrangements for a flight the next day. Also, I needed to get someone to run the boat, since I didn't know how long I would be gone.

Vance, my son, could take care of the business, if he would. He could be the mate and hire a captain when he booked a charter. I checked with Vance that night. He agreed to run the *Miss Gina*. Now I could go.

After the funeral, we discussed whether or not I would want to live in South Padre Island. We would have a house on a canal paid for. I could move the *Miss Gina* to South Padre. It was also paid for. My decision had nothing to do with the house and the boat. It had to do with the entire layout of the island. So. Padre Island is located on the southern tip of Texas, next to Mexico. There are few trees and not much other vegetation besides cactus. Mostly it is sandy beaches. There are hotels, bars, and restaurants, but a small full time population.

Fishing in the Gulf of Mexico is not even close to fishing in the Gulf Stream. The Gulf of Mexico is shaped like a large soup bowl. Shallow water for up to sixty miles from shore, then it gets deep very slowly. For me, to take the kind of trips I was used to, I'd have to run one hundred and twenty miles round trip. At fifteen knots, that would take eight hours. There would be not time for fishing.

Carol had no family. She could live anywhere. I had my son and my father living in Key West, so, I said no to South Padre Island.

When all the details, such as fixing and renting the house were done, we decided to buy a new pick up truck and tow the Jeep back to Key West. It took us two weeks. We stopped at every little town, took all the side roads, and even stopped at one of my charter's houses for a few days.

Chapter 19.
Suicide Attempt, Stuart Is The Mate

I've been told a lot of stories as to why the mates can't make it to the boat on time for a charter. Victor's "no show" one day, caused me to fire him and hire another mate. The day Victor missed, he said he had the flu but someone saw him the night before so drunk he could hardly stand. This was called the brown bottle flue.

Once, when Vance was my mate, he showed up late for a charter with the excuse that someone broke into his house and shut off his alarm clock! Mates don't seem to stay employed on one boat for more than one season. Our season starts at Christmas and goes on until Memorial Day.

My next mate was Stuart. He was a small framed guy, five feet six inches tall and one hundred forty pounds, with black hair and a goatee. Stuart had fished on charter boats in Virginia Beach, Virginia, as well as Key West for the last five years.

Stuart got a single man to charter the boat for an afternoon half. I came to the boat at noon. Stuart had the boat ready, the man was ready, so off we went. The man said he just wanted to get out on the water for a while. On a four hour trip, there is not much time to go any distance, so I went to the reef first to catch barracuda, yellow tail, or grouper. After that, I headed south to deeper water, about one hundred to two hundred feet to see what might be there. After trolling awhile, I noticed Stuart blowing up a small life ring, like kids use in the home pool.

I asked Stuart, "What is that and what is he going to do with it?"

Stuart came up to the bridge to talk to me. He explained the customer wanted to get off shore far enough so we couldn't see land. He had never been out that far before. I told Stuart there wouldn't be any fish that deep at this time of year. Stuart said he had told the man that, but the man didn't care. As I went farther and farther south, I was thinking we were going to be seven miles from Key West to the reef, then seven or eight miles past the reef. I wondered what could be the real reason we were going out this far. I asked Stuart to ask the gentleman to come up on the bridge with me.

I asked the man, who was in his mid forties, "What is going on?"

He asked me, "What would you do if I wanted to commit suicide?" He wanted to take his life ring and jump off the boat.

I explained, "I will get the gaff and stick it in your ass and pull you back in the boat, because there is too much paper work to fill out for the Coast Guard!"

He told me that he figured this would be the cleanest way to commit suicide. There would be no blood, no mess, and no friends or relatives who would be shocked when they found him dead at home.

We chatted about the subject for a half hour. I persuaded him to wait and see if things would be better tomorrow. Back at the dock, he showed me he had a duffel bag full of chains and a lead ball, as well as a pistol. What he was going to do was take a boat out to deep water (five hundred or six hundred feet), get into his life ring, and wrap the chains and lead ball around himself, get into the water, puncture the life ring, and shoot himself in the head. The body would go down, and out of sight in a few seconds.

After that explanation, I said, "Let me take you back to your motel."

He told me he had no more money. He had spent his last three hundred dollars for this trip. I asked, "What about a tip for the mate?"

He said, "I didn't think about that because I wasn't coming back."

We made an agreement that I would loan him sixty dollars for the motel, twenty-five dollars for the tip, and twenty dollars to eat supper. We would meet tomorrow morning at Fisherman's Cafe for breakfast and by then he could wire for money to repay me.

The next morning, I went to the cafe to see if he would appear or not. He did. We ate, he repaid the loan, and was in much better spirits. I never saw or heard from him again and have often wondered what happened to him.

Chapter 20.
Fun Trip on the Cha Cha With Johnny, Tony, & Manny

Sitting at the dock talking with the fellow captains while we waited for cars to pass the boats to book a charter, we discussed past trips. It was just like truck drivers at the coffee shop talked trucks, or oil field workers discussed where they were when the well blew out.

Johnny Potter took a boat to Cuba in 1981, when Castro let a lot of people leave the country. Most of these people were from Mariel prison. On his way over, he hit a storm. The waves were so big, one of them came over the bow of the boat and broke out the front windows of his vessel. After that, he stopped three different times to rescue other boats that had run out of fuel or had mechanical breakdowns. The people got on Johnny's boat and tied their boats behind his. After completing the ninety mile trip, through wind, rain, and high seas, he missed the entrance to Marina Hemingway, which is twenty miles west of Havana. One of his passengers told him he needed to go back to the east. So, for another hour they cruised the Cuban coast east till they found the marina entrance. Still, this was not bad. Johnny was only seventeen years old then, and had never left the island of Key West before.

Owners and captains enjoy fishing and adventures, too. One day, the owners of the last three boats at my end of the dock, Johnny Potter, Anthony Saldono, and I were talking about the recent influx of yellow fin tuna. This was an unusual event in these waters, because our water is normally too warm for yellow fin tuna to come this far south. A lot of them are caught in the Bahamas. For the past week, many yellow fins weighing from seventy-five to one hundred and fifty pounds had been caught off Key West.

Johnny had been nipping on his bottle of Captain Morgan's, I had had a couple of beers, but Anthony didn't drink, so , we had one competent captain. A big Spanish young man called Manny happened to be standing around with us while we were deciding whether to try our luck catching a big yellow fin.

Johnny said we could take his boat. His wife wouldn't mind spending the money for fuel if she got a big slice of fresh tuna for Sushi. We all agreed. Anthony would be captain. Manny and I would be mates. That left Johnny to do what Johnny wanted to do, which was give orders. We gathered what we needed bait, ice, four eighty pound rods and reels, and sandwiches. Within thirty minutes we were ready to go out in pursuit of large game fish again.

We cast off and headed to Key West harbor. After a massive amount of discussion, we decided to go southeast, out to the wall (the wall is where the water depth drops off fast to one thousand feet). Seven miles from the harbor, at the SE Channel Marker, Johnny threw his emptied bottle of Captain Morgan's over the side. Cruising at fifteen knots, the forty-five foot, twin diesel engine, *Cha Cha*, takes an hour to arrive at the trolling depth of eight hundred feet. We put out artificial bait, large Cona heads that pop and splash. Two lines were short, about twenty-five feet behind the boat. Two lines were longer, eighty to one hundred feet behind.

We started at ten o'clock, now it was eleven. The most time we can give this trip is until two o'clock because we all need to book our boats for tomorrow. Once we got to the wall, we had only two choices, go south or go west, due to the

Gulf Stream moving to the east with a three to five knot current. It can take us too far east, away from home.

Anthony decided to go west, zig zagging north and south to get different depths of water from eight hundred to twelve hundred feet.

Someone once said, "Trolling is hours of pure boredom interrupted by moments of sheer terror". I have found this to be very true.

We had more years of fishing experience on this boat than on any other charter boat in the gulf stream that day. Johnny is twenty-five years old. He started working on boats when he was six years old. He would come down to the fishing docks in the afternoon with his mother and father and help wash boats. Anthony graduated from Key West High School, then went to college to become a pharmacist. A land job was not for him. Fishing was in his blood. At thirty-five years old, he had owned a charter boat for twelve years. Manny has been a mate up and down the dock for anyone that needed a mate part time for ten years. His size is impressive. At six feet one inch, two hundred sixty-five pounds, he would be handy on board when we catch the one hundred seventy-five pound yellow fin tuna, because we do not have a tuna door. (A tuna door is a cut out in the transom, which makes the deck level with the water.) I was the old man of the crew. At that time, my age was forty-five. I had been fishing for six years, and was in good physical shape at six feet tall, two hundred-five pounds.

We listened to the VHF radio to hear if we were close to anyone who had caught any yellow fin. We heard that three tuna were hooked up not far away. We checked the Loran and headed that direction. All of a sudden there was a huge splash behind the left long rigger. The splash was so big it looked like someone dropped a Volkswagen into the water. All of us waited to hear the reel start to sing from the clicking. Two minutes passed, five minutes, nothing. A swing and a miss, so we waited for the next one.

I took over the wheel. It was time to think about heading home. Anthony sits in the fighting chair, drinking a coke. Johnny tells me to go south. I said, "Let's go north, towards home".

He said, "I want a fish, let's stay out longer. You're fired! Get up. I'm driving!"

I got up in time to hear one of the reels start that beautiful sound, "Click, Click, Click" at fifty miles per hour. Manny picked up the rod and stuck it into the gimble of the fighting chair. Anthony took over. Johnny hit the throttles just a short punch to set the hook. Manny and I reeled in the remaining three rods. Anthony was pulling up and winding down, just like he knew what he was doing. Of course, Johnny was jelling, "bring in the other lines, get the gaff!"

I yelled back, "Shut up!"

He said, "you're fired!"

I replied, "I'm already fired!"

Anthony was doing a great job at whipping the fish. In twenty minutes he had the fish to the boat. Manny leaned over the side with the gaff and sticks the fish behind the head. Gaffing was one of the hardest things to learn how to do. If you stick the fish too far behind the head, you don't have any control, also the fillet has a hole in it. Right behind the head is the perfect place to hit the fish. This yellow fin tuna was not the one we were hoping for, but big enough, about seventy-five pounds. Johnny's skills at the helm, and Anthony's tenacious angling skills got us a tuna in record time. Retrieving a large fish quickly is important. A lot can happen while it is hooked and in the water, such as: another fish with teeth can cut the monofiliment line or bite the fish, or floating pallet or board can cut the line.

We had our fish in the boat. Everyone was happy.

Sushi tonight!

Chapter 21.
Purchase of the Ms. Gina

Through the years of discussing things with Red about fishing trips to Cuba and the Dry Tortugas (islands sixty miles west of Key West that house Fort Jefferson, a National Park and a marinesanctuary), I learned that if I wanted to do this type of overnight charter we needed a larger boat. It would handle more smoothly in rough weather and high seas. In the winter, it would give me more trips, which would help make the payments.

Fidel Castro had taken over Cuba in 1959. It was 1991, and tensions had eased. There was a group called Basta in Key West that was trying to give humanitarian aid to the Cuban people. Since 1959, the United States government put an embargo on Cuba so nothing was sold to

Cuba from the United States. At this time, travel to Cuba is frowned upon nor can a United States citizen, except for the press, spend money in Cuba. The press is allowed to spend one hundred dollars per day. By joining Basta there was a chance I could meet the right people, help in their effort, and take a trip to Cuba. That was another reason for getting a bigger, faster boat. John Young was the president of the group and Wayne Kruer was the lawyer for Basta. Wayne spoke fluent Spanish and had been a basketball coach in Spain for several years before he moved to Key West.

Now it was time to talk to my financier, Carol. We discussed the pros and cons of another boat. We decided the cost of this vessel should not be over one hundred thousand dollars. We would also need another slip to keep the boat in or sell the *Miss Gina*. I started searching in various boating periodicals and newspapers for a boat that would meet my needs.

The Miami Herald Newspaper is a good source for used vessels. We found a broker in there that had a 1974 Jersey, with twin 671 Detroit Diesel engines, that was forty feet long and had a sixteen foot beam. The broker gave me the details on the boat called *The Phantom* at the time. I got hold of Ed, a friend that is a boat right and also a good mechanic. He and I took the trip to Ft. Lauderdale that was also a vacation from the rock (Key West is called the rock by the locals). It was about a three and a half hour drive. The boat was docked at the Bahia Mar Hotel Marina in Ft. Lauderdale, at the Charter Boat Row.

Ed and I boarded the vessel. Opening the engine hatch, we discovered this boat had been neglected for a while. One engine smoked and there was oil in the bilge. The salon had chairs, carpet, and drapes that were in good shape: also some of the appliances needed to be thrown away, such as the freezer. The door was total rust, plus it added a lot of weight that we did not need.

Ed and I left the dock to eat, and then take the long ride home. During this time we discussed the pros and cons of *The Phantom*. The engines were old but Detroit 671's were easy to gets parts for and most mechanics are used to working on them. The cockpit was smaller than I liked but the fighting chair was very expensive and in good shape. The boat had an old generator and air conditioning which I wanted in the new boat. The fly bridge was large and well appointed with benches to seat four people comfortably as well as a nice steering station for the helms person. The conclusion was it was basically solid and with some tender love and care, she would make a great charter boat, at the right price!

Upon return, I got with Carol and had more discussions. We agreed on no more than fifty thousand dollars. On Thanksgiving eve, the broker called and asked if I would give forty-five thousand dollars?

I said, "No."

He asked, "Would you give twenty-five thousand dollars?"

I said, "Yes."

He said, "Fine, we will split the difference, thirty-seven, five."

I said, "OK, that's a deal."

He requested a check faxed to him and said he would set up the documentation transfer.

After Carol and I drove the boat back to the Keys, we had our work cut out for us, as well as Ed had a lot to take care of too.

I decided to rename *The Phantom*, *Ms. Gina.* Phantom sounded too negative for me. Something that exists but has no physical reality is not what I want to go fishing on. Besides all my advertisement was in the *Miss Gina* name.

Chapter 22.
Fun Trip to Boca Grande on Ms. Gina

After having a semi successful first spring with the *Ms. Gina*, I decided to take Carol on a fun fishing trip to Boca Grande on the west coast of Florida. Ed, a friend and mechanic who helped us service and repair our new acquisition, also went with us. He also liked to navigate. Having a third party on board keeps people from confrontation that two might have. Before leaving on this one hundred-fifty mile trip, I asked Red what to look for. He told me about the days when he used to take charters to the Shark River, which is located a little north of the Everglades and south of Naples on the west corner of Florida. The river is fifty feet wide with mangroves growing out of the water concealing the waters edge of the bank. This type of fishing is completely different from trolling or live baiting for sailfish .It's fly casting or chumming, using cut mullet on large hooks.

At certain times in the year, large tarpon would retreat to the estuaries to spawn. Other techniques were used to catch spotted trout or red fish.

From Key West to the Everglades National Park is only fifty or sixty miles, then a few more miles to the Shark River. It was at least a two-day trip in Red's day because they had a forty foot cruiser with a single engine. We would be much faster. We gathered charts at Key West Marine Hardware Store. It was called the candy store because they had everything for the fisherman and boaters. I had a thirty-day account, so the price was no object until the end of the month when the bill came due.

Charts are navigational aids-like maps for land people. On the charts are signs and symbols marking the channels, as well as the depths of water and loran numbers in different directions so you can pinpoint your location. Carol and Ed love this navigation stuff. I, on the other hand, am a fly-by-the-seat-of-my-pants type of guy, but you notice I have two navigators on board.

Taking a long trip, you need a lot of preparation-food, drinking water, beer, and soda for three people for five days, extra oil, a fan belt-just in case, check the anchor and line, bait for fishing, five hundred pounds of ice (it melts fast at ninety degree days). We had to take our two dogs: mine was Boogie, a black lab, and Snowflake, a cocker spaniel that Carol had had for years. Both dogs were boat trained; they only pooped or piddled in the cockpit in emergencies. It could be washed down with the hose quite easily while underway.

We headed out Northwest Channel early in the morning on another great adventure or as my friend Johnny Potter would say, "a fun filled, action packed adventure." He also would say, "Were going to do some deep sea drinking."

The Gulf of Mexico is shaped like a large soup bowl, shallow along the edges and deep in the middle. From Key West north for thirty miles, the water is only thirty feet deep, and then gets slightly deeper every mile as you go north.

It's my boat and I was driving, but I steer like a fisherman, zigging and zagging to the left then to the right. The boat is going at fifteen knots, so what's an extra mile or three in the trip? The navigators plot our location every hour and then I'd catch hell because we were too far west or east. They would tell me "follow the compass heading we give you." So, I would let either Carol or Ed take the wheel for a while and

I'd eat or drink a beer. It took us ten hours to get to Boca Grande. Along the way, we saw porpoise playing in our bow and stern wake. They seem to have a lot of fun doing this. We also saw a shark's dorsal fin sticking about six inches out of the water.

The water in the Gulf of Mexico isn't clear like it is in the gulf stream. The clearest it gets is an emerald green. The visibility is only a few feet.

Reaching our destination of Boca Grande, we see ten or fifteen small runabout skiffs milling around in the harbor entrance, not leaving much room for the largest, *Ms. Gina*, to pass. The people were fishing for tarpon. They are quite an exciting fish to catch. As soon as the fish feel the hook in their mouth sticking them, they jump out of the water, leaping eight or ten feet. We slowed down, leaving no wake, so we did not swamp any of the smaller vessels. This is the polite thing to do, as well as it's the law. A vessel is responsible for it's wake. Cruising slowly into the open area of the harbor, we found an uninhabited area where we could anchor. Close by, there was a sandy beach where we could take the dogs to shore in our dingy.

The next morning, after checking our charts, we devised a plan. We would go to Fort Myers Beach for a day, then Shark River for a day, and

Everglades National Park for a day. After that, it's only fifty miles back to Key West.

This trip took five days. I learned a lot about navigating to distant places, and entering new rivers and marinas. I had been on charter boats for eight years, always going out of Key West and returning to the same place, never using charts or plotting a course.

Chapter 23.
Red's Sea Adventures Talking with Vance & Bud

Even though Vance and I didn't work together, we still went downtown to see Red, my father and Vance's grandfather. We would sit at the corner barrel, just to the right, as you came in the door of the Bull. The building stands at the corner of Caroline and Duvall Street. It was erected sometime in the late eighteen hundreds. The Bull and The Whistle Bar were my father's hangouts. Red quit drinking some time ago, but he still liked to socialize in the afternoon at the bar. He would bring his newspaper and sit at the same place every day.

The seating decor in The Bull was old whiskey barrels for tables and four chairs at each barrel. The bar itself was in the shape of the state of Florida. When you entered the bar, you were geographically at Mobile, Alabama. The locals would generally sit around Panama City or Tallahassee.

The three generations would talk about the day's events, or ask the old man about fishing, such as locations of wrecks in the Gulf, or where the German submarine was sunk and how it got there. Red had also been a hard-hat diver for the Coast Guard and The Western Union Co.

Red would tell us about current events that he had read in the day's paper. I wanted to know about the past and heritage. Vance couldn't stop watching the girls walking down the street long enough to hear anything about what his forty-five year old father or his seventy-five year old grandfather were saying.

Captain Red quit the sea when he was fifty-four years old and with a master's license unlimited. This is the biggest license the US Coast Guard issues.

The Western Union Co. laid cable underground on the island of Key West. They put the cable in long wooden coffins so the line would not be cut by the coral rock. When they got to the beach they kept going by ship to Cuba. Hard-hat divers were required to make sure the cable didn't get caught on the coral heads or ship wrecks. Captain Red did this till the job was completed. A large sailing ship called *The Western Union* carried the cable. The last time I was in Key West, January, 2000, the ship was docked behind The Schooner Wharf, a local bar at Key West Bight.

During W.W.II, German submarines would travel the east coast of the United States. They came as far south as Key West. One of the subs was captured and sank off Key West. It still lies in two pieces, twenty miles west of the harbor in two hundred feet of water.

There are all kinds of sunken ships around Key West because of the shallow waters and treacherous reef just off shore. Fish use these wrecks as their home. Now, finding these wrecks is easy with the new GPS (Global Positioning System) navigation and a chart of the area. When I was fishing, the loran navigation system was used to locate the wreck. Loran systems picked up radio waves from sending towers on land and calculated the distance you were from them and gave you a digital read out of your latitude and longitude. In my fathers day, word of mouth passed on the location of the wrecks. You would be told a compass course out of the harbor, then the depth of the water, and to look towards shore and line up the two radio towers with the tall building or other line of sight objects. When you found the wreck you could generally count on finding good eating fish to catch in the area. Another trick the captains used was to drop a length of rope tied to a stick of soap. They would let the soap hit the bottom, pull it back up, and check to see what kind of bottom was down there. A rocky bottom is a good bottom to fish over.

During the forties the US Coast Guard recruited men from Key West and the Florida Keys to be pilots for the military shipping in the area, due to their knowledge of the waters. All local boatmen, because of his deeds, knew Red. After the 1935 hurricane in the Florida Keys, Red ran the hospital ship. The ship cruised around the islands picking up the injured and dead. In the thirties the only way to travel was by train or ship. The train tracks were destroyed by the high water and wind that exceeded one hundred miles per hour.

At the time of the 1935 hurricane, the Captain was twenty-six years old. He started working on boats at seventeen years old, so in thirty-five he had nine years of experience. Legal age to get a captain's license is eighteen years old. After a few years on merchant ships, and a few years on local boats he took the written test about the rules of the road (or sea), safety procedures, and fire fighting. He passed the test and got a fifty-ton operator's license. Then, after more years of sea service on bigger fishing boats and another test, he qualified for a two hundred ton license. (It is legal for a person to operate a vessel without a license, if there are no paying passengers on board.) After a lot of years working on all sorts of vessels, Red qualified for a Masters License Unlimited. This means he could operate any ship on any waters in the world.

He went to work at Delmonico's Bar in the early sixties as a night watchman. Once a man on the outside of the fence, who wanted to rob the place, shot him in the back. The neighbors called the police. The man was caught and sent to prison. My father got well with no after effects.

What would you think if you saw your grandfather riding a bicycle down the street with a known hooker on the handlebars? Vance encountered this situation one evening just about dark. He was coming out of Delmonico's, just in time to see this event in progress. Vance told me he didn't think his grandfather was giving her a lift to the grocery store. I told Vance, that Red said, "If you don't use it, you lose it!"

Being a bouncer/watchman in a gay bar in the sixties, seventies, and eighties was a rough job. It was only the last of the rough jobs Red had had during his life.

While at sea three different boats burned out from under him.

Once he was in the water for seventy-two hours before he was rescued. The boat he was running caught on fire in the engine room. With no way to put out the fire, Red and the crew grabbed their life jackets and jumped into the water.. The boat burned and sank. They bobbed around for several days. A large dolphin kept bumping Red with his nose for hours making black and blue marks all over his body. After seventy-two hours a shrimp boat rescued them and took them back to shore.

Half of his thumb was missing because of a shark bite. The story told at the dock, said that Red was helping another crew member out of the water when a shark came up. He got the man out but lost his thumb.

He walked with a limp because of a stroke when he was in his fifties.

In his later years, a cab hit him while he was riding his bicycle. He always rode a bicycle around town (he never got a driver's license for a car). As he got older, his skills at this decreased and the streets are very narrow. The cab was passing him and he swerved into the cab. We know this because the dent was on the side of the cab. Red was knocked down. His elbows and knees were skinned. The lady passenger was upset. She was about sixty-five years old. Red told the cab driver in no uncertain terms to take the "OLD" lady home because he was fine. He gave the driver a piece of his mind and peddled on. He was eighty-one at the time.

Fortunately, he was never hurt so badly that he did not recover and work another day.

Red had three great loves in his life: women, young children, and animals. During the years, Key West attracted people from all over the country, getting away from it all. When young women were down on their luck, they always knew there was a place to stay with Red. Quite a few of these women had small children and they were welcome. While the women "got their act together" if Red was not working, he would baby-sit for the kids. He also fed all the stray dogs and cats in the neighborhood. As he got older and the kids grew up, they still continued to stop by and see that Captain Red was OK. Several of the women he helped when they were all much younger, continued to keep in touch and when he was in his eighties they saw that he got to the doctor, or any other assistance he might need.

Red had a favorite dog named Boogie. He was a stray like all the rest, but stayed with Red wherever he went. Boogie had learned Red's routine so well that he would wake him up when it was time to go to work. Once, when Boogie was waiting for Red outside a restaurant, the dogcatcher captured him. They took Boogie to the dog pound in Marathon, Florida. Since Marathon is fifty miles north of Key West, Red had to ask a friend to drive him up there to get Boogie out of jail. On their way back, Red's friend said they should have bought property years ago and they would have made a fortune. Red said they didn't have any money then, either.

Captain Red was well known on Duvall Street, due to his longevity. He was born in the two-story, red brick house on Caroline Street just off Duvall, in 1909, which is a bar named after him.

From 1909 until 1989 he lived and hung out in the same three or four block area, when he wasn't at sea. He only left Key West to commercial fish, sport fish with Hemingway and others in the thirties, and then, piloting for the Coast Guard during W.W.II.

Commercial fishing takes a person who likes to be alone for days at a time. Sometimes a mate comes along, if you can find someone who is fun to be with for three or four days at a time. The catch depends on the time of year. In the winter it could be king mackerel. In the summer is could be yellow tail snapper. Making money depends on the fish biting.

Sport fishing is mostly day trips. Sometimes you do an overnight trip. You take from one to six people. You get paid for the charter even if no fish are caught. There are a lot of people on the boat and they are asking a lot of questions.

When the war was over Key West was poor. No work, or no tourists. Red, like many of us, drank too much when he got depressed. The late fifties and early sixties were better. He ran a tugboat from Ft. Lauderdale to Puerto Rico pushing fuel barges. By 1967, he had had enough of the sea, and decided it was time to get a land job. He worked at the same bar, which changed hands seven times, until his eightieth birthday.

Red's birthday was July 14, 1909. July 14, is also Bastille Day which is when the French freed the prisoners during the French Revolution. The combination of Bastille Day and Red's birthday called for an annual party. There were three bars that would always ask if they could have the party at their place. Red quit drinking at sixty but he still went to the bars to socialize with old friends. This small framed, slim, white haired, old man that walked with a limp and drug his left foot with every other step was much loved by all in this four block area.

Three bars each wanted the party at their place. The Bull faced Duvall Street and is on the corner of Caroline and Duval. Two doors west was the building Red was born in. It was a bar called Red's Place. The third bar was The Whistle. It was located over the Bull. The Bull and the Whistle were owned and managed by the same person. The Ramos family leased the house where Red was born to Pat and he turned it into a bar. He was a big man with a loud booming voice. It became a popular local hang out and featured one dollar draft beer. Even though he stopped drinking years before, Red had a permanent seat of honor there. Red's Place was a real drunk's bar. The kind that sells a lot of dollar drafts and you can see junk hanging from the walls and ceiling. Not too many tourists found their way into Red's. They usually passed by quickly. On the other hand, the Bull catered to tourists as well as the Whistle with its pool tables and electronic games.

About a month before the birthday the owners would see me having a drink in their place and suggest the party be at their place. I tried to move it from place to place each year. The owners wanted the party because in July there were few tourists. Only the locals were drinking and the party would bring in a lot of money. The food and cake would be provided by me and the other guests, like a pot luck, but everyone bought their own drinks at the bar.

The corner of Caroline and Duvall Streets was a gathering place for street people and panhandlers. Some were Viet Nam veterans with missing body parts and others just drank too much. There were a few that were real characters. A guy called Feathers who had long brown hair that hadn't been washed or combed for months, wore a ball cap pulled down tight over his hair. In the small vent holes of his hat he stuck feathers of all kinds: pelican, sea gull, sand pipers, whatever he found. Feathers carried a worn out broom and would sweep the side walk outside the Bull. If you struck up a conversation with him he would ask if you would like to hear a joke. If the answer was yes the price was three jokes for a dollar.

I showed up at the Bull late one afternoon after a charter. I had a pocket full of money and a belly full of beer. As I got out of my pickup, a young man about twenty that was standing on the side walk, said "Hi Bud". I said "Hi, come on in and I will buy you a drink". This guy had a metal ring around his head with two braces extending down from the ring to his shoulders. I noticed there were four screws going through the ring into the skin and hair. After I offered the drink he said, "No, I have more money than you do". We both got out our wads of money and counted them out. I started with one hundred, two hundred, till I got to seven hundred-twenty dollars. When he was finished counting he had nine hundred-thirty dollars. I said, "Well you win. The drinks are on you." We went inside the Bull and I asked about his cranial attachment. He told me that he broke his neck and the jewelry had to stay on his head for six months but it didn't stop us having several cold beers.

There were many characters that knew Red and on his birthday they would all show up at the party. It was fun to see some of the kids he had baby sat for there with children of their own.

One year when the party was at Red's Place I brought a large ham and a huge bowl of potato salad. Others had brought large bowls of salsa and chips, Cuban mix sandwiches, key lime pie, mangos, and other great things to eat. The food sat on a large folding table inside the bar over in the corner. The ladies finished uncovering the goodies and placing the paper plates and napkins. I went to the bar to get another beer and visit with a few friends. When I returned a short time later the food was all gone. So much for free food.

Until his death, his birthday party was attended by hundreds of people of all ages who knew and loved him.

Some of the people that cared deeply for Captain Red were Charlie Ramos and his family. These people gave my father a place to work for twenty years as a night watchman at the bar. A.J. owned Shorty's Diner on Duval Street for thirty years and my father never paid for a meal. All the bar owners at Red's Place, The Bull, Rick's, and Sloppy Joe's new and loved the captain.

Red helped many young people who were down on their luck. He was also friendly to the many fishermen and boat people through the years.

Chapter 24.
Victor, Ms. Gina, & Picking Up a Scuba Diver

The most unusual fish I ever caught at the jetties was a scuba diver.

Since March is such a windy month and a lot of people still want to go fishing, the charter boats have different directions they could go when they leave the harbor every day. If the wind was blowing out of the Northeast, I would go to the Gulf of Mexico. To get there, I cruised out Northwest Channel for eight miles. We would fish for barracuda, jack cravel, and sometimes bluefish, along a man-made reef we called jetties. This area was good to get some action, not large game fish, but a great place for small children and first time fishermen to have some fun on a windy day.

Victor and I chartered a couple and their ten-year-old son. Going to the Gulf is a little different from going to the Atlantic. You still go under the Garrison Bight bridge, that's a must. At Fleming Key, we had a choice of going under the bridge or going around the island to troll for barracuda on the way, which we did. Once in Key West Harbor, we headed west to Northwest Channel, going between Tank and Wisteria Island which used to be called Shark Island in my father's day because they killed and cleaned sharks to sell for their livers. It takes thirty to forty-five minutes if you don't run aground. The channel is well marked. Red day-markers are on your left, green ones are on the right. "Red-right-returning" is the saying for boaters to know how to go through channels. It means red markers are to be kept on the right (starboard) side of the boat when you are going from a larger body of water into a smaller body of water.

We arrived at the south end of the jetties that was marked by large rocks protruding out of the water. Out went the baits, the deep troll last, because the water was only three to five feet deep. This was a location we, the Conchs or native guides liked best to fish on an incoming tide. Women and children fish first on my boat. The wife and son each caught barracudas. Dad got a nice jack cravel. By now, we were close to the end of their half-day charter. It's time to turn around. While turning, I look towards the West. I see a green can buoy about two hundred yards away, leaning at a forty-five degree angle. I called Victor up to the bridge to get his opinion.

I asked, "What's wrong with that buoy?"

He said, "It's the current making it lean so much."

I said, "Bring in the lines and let's go see."

After a five-minute cruise towards the buoy, we saw that a person had climbed up onto the buoy. When we got to the man, he was dressed in a black wet suit, scuba tank, and carrying a large net bag.

I asked if he called for a taxi!

He answered, " Yes, a long time ago!"

We bow up close to the buoy and Victor helped him aboard. After he removed his gear and got a drink, he explained the situation. He had hired a guy to drive his small ski boat and stay close to his bubble trail as he searched the bottom for lobster. He supposed the current had taken him faster than the boat driver anticipated and lost track of him. When he surfaced, there was no boat and driver... He grabbed onto the buoy before he was swept into the Gulf of Mexico. As we were coming back, all eyes searched for the little boat and saw nothing.

After we tied up at the dock, I told the guy he would have to pay for his return trip.

He said, "Sure, anything."

I said, "I needed four lobster."

"Cheap enough", he replied.

Chapter 25.
Conch Tour of Key West & Changing the Oil

If, by ten or eleven in the morning, no one had comes to charter the boat it was time to make a decision. Should we take the day off and do some maintenance and have a few beers or continue to wait for a charter?

While sitting at the dock, time is spent working on the boat, repairing broken rods and reels, and re-spooling reels with line that was lost on previous trips. It is imperative that the line on every reel be full of new line, because the day may come that the biggest fish will hit the bait on the reel that has the least line. When he takes that run at sixty miles per hour for one minute, and you hear "POW" that sounds like a twenty-two rifle being fired, a sickening feeling comes over everyone. The next thing someone says is, "I wonder what kind of fish that was?"

Changing the oil and filters on the engines can be an all day job. Gathering filters and oil means taking a trip all the way to Stock Island, which is five miles away. When the mate and I take that long trip, we must stop at Che Che's Bar for a twelve-pack to go. (Che Che's is a long time hang out for locals. My mother started working there in 1941 before W.W.II.) Now, primed for a great task, our commodities in hand, we made a five mile trip into an eight or nine mile trip. The speed limit in Key West is thirty miles per hour. We went down Truman Avenue to Duvall Street, took a right towards the Gulf of Mexico to see who was at the Bull, then over to Rick's, across the street past Sloppy Joe's, and down to the Ocean Key House. We turned around in the Pier House parking lot and went south. At the light, we took a right and went five blocks, checked out who was at the Green Parrot, only stopping if it was necessary to relieve our kidneys or to see someone we knew. Next, we went north on United Street towards the beach to see the girls in string bikinis playing volleyball. While going slowly along the busy beach street, Victor hung out the window of my pick up truck to say "thank you" to a lovely lady wearing a bright orange two-piece bikini. We proceeded to Stock Island. It was lunch time, so we went to the Rusty Anchor Restaurant for fried shrimp and a cold beer to wash them down.

After gathering our supplies at the Marine Hardware Store, back to the boat we went. It took about ten minutes, and that was stopping at two red lights. We changed the oil-five gallons in each of two engines, replaced four filters, two oil filters, and two fuel filters, and cleaned up the mess. It was time for a beer that was kept in the freezer where we kept the bait.

So far today, I had gotten up, put on my T shirt, shorts, and deck shoes. Grabbed my hat and sunglasses to go to the boat. On the way I stopped to get a coffee con leche (Cuban coffee with hot milk and sugar). I sat at the dock chatting with Tony Saldono and Johnny Potter (two boat owners and captains of the *Reef Runner* and the *Cha Cha* respectively). Victor and I took a Conch tour of the island. I was tired and hot. We needed a rest. Off we went to Schooner Wharf Bar located in Key West Bight. The shrimp boats used to dock there when I was a young man. Now, it had a bar and band stand. Michael McCloud was entertaining. My favorite of his songs was the Conch Republic Song. One of the lines in this song is "I'd rather be here drinking a beer than freezing my ass off in the north".

I got home late and went straight to bed. The phone ringing woke me at ten thirty the next morning.

A woman's voice said, "Bud, you didn't pay your rent. Why?"

In my foggy sleeping state I had to think who was talking to me. Oh, it's the lady I rent this house from. She and her husband moved to Key West a few years ago. They retired from the carnival and bought rental properties. Since I was not usually late on my rent, she must be checking to see if something was wrong. Knowing her as a friend as well as landlady, I knew she had a good sense of humor. Both she and her husband fished regularly and understood my business.

I said, "I had to celebrate". She wanted to know what the occasion was. I told her I had changed the oil and filters in the boat.

She asked, "Is that something to celebrate?"

"Yes," I said, "It only happens on the first of every month, and that means I am still in business."

"Good," she exclaimed, "bring me the rent, today!"

Chapter 26.
Dry Tortugas on the Ms. Gina

Another trip I took with Carol was to the Dry Tortugas. We had been there once with the little *Miss Gina*. On this trip, we met Johnny Potter and his mate Derrick Stirup. Johnny always took Derrick because he was a good cook that knew how to fish. They were both Conchs, born and raised in Key West. These islands were their back yard. Most Conchs start fishing and boating at an early age, about the same time country boys start hunting rabbits and learning how to shoot a rifle.

Before starting on any trip I took time to go downtown to see Red and ask about the trip at hand. There are a string of islands in between Key West and the Dry Tortugas. Tank Island, located in Key West Harbor, is the first.

Heading west from there, you pass Man Key, Woman Key, The Marquesses, one and on, until you reach Rebecca Shoal Light. Captain Red suggested that if the wind is blowing from the south, which is the prevailing direction in the summer, you travel on the north or leeward side of the islands. Doing it this way, the islands decrease the effect of the wind and seas on your vessel. The same thing is true in reverse; the winds are prevailing from the north, so travel on the south side of the islands. Also, the water is shallow close to the islands on the Gulf side.

I didn't need to talk to the Captain about this trip, I had Carol. She studied the charts until she was confident about where she was going, but going downtown was fun. Seeing Red, talking to the locals, having a few beers, and visiting with the tourists is all in a day's work. Besides, I might meet someone who wants to charter the boat.

Again, taking any trip, it is the preparation before hand that makes the trip safe and pleasant. I liked living in the pleasant. Since we run the *Ms. Gina* one hundred-fifty to two hundred days a year, we keep a close eye on our maintenance, so mostly it's getting food, ice, and beer. Going to the Dry Tortugas is at least a three-day trip or longer. On any trip out in the ocean, the rule is to bring too much--you will use it the next trip. We load up with two-hundred dollars in food and six-hundred pounds of ice.

It was summer when we left, so it's out Northwest Channel past the Hemingway Tower, a tower that once had a small house on top, located at the end of the NW Channel. It was told that Ernest Hemingway went there to write. The wood structure burned but the metal frame is still standing. We continue another three or four miles until the depth gauge indicates we are traveling in at least thirty feet of water. From there we head west past the islands, Rebecca Shoal Light, and on to Fort Jefferson in the Dry Tortugas. It took us about four hours.

Ponce De Leon originally discovered these seven tiny islands in 1513. The islands were named the Dry Tortugas because they had abundant sea turtles (Tortugas in Spanish) for food but no fresh water (thus dry) to supply the passing ships. In 1825 our government erected a navigational light and in 1846, Fort Jefferson construction was started. In those days, the location was strategic, protecting the Gulf of Mexico trade. Construction went on for thirty years. The fort was never completed, but it was used as a Northern prison during and after the Civil War. Dr. Samuel Mudd, convicted of complicity in President Lincoln's assassination, was its most famous prisoner. The islands were named a wildlife refuge to protect nesting birds in 1908. In 1935, Fort Jefferson was named a national monument. The Dry Tortugas and Fort Jefferson were named a national park in 1992.

The beauty and history of the Dry Tortugas draws people to visit this hard-to-get-to place. You must come by boat or fly in by seaplane. There are no supplies there so you must be self-contained. The trip is well worth the effort. Bird watching, snorkeling, and fishing are spectacular. We spent several days enjoying the area and eating fresh fish.

If you were to charter my boat in those days to go to the Dry Tortugas it would have cost one thousand dollars per day for up to six guests. Sure, there are cheaper fishing trips in small open fishing boats with no head (the head is the rest room, bathroom, or lue). Instead, it's a five-gallon bucket emptied over the side. On my boat, it was hot meals, air-conditioned cabin, hot shower, and a nice soft bed while listening to the lap of the waves on the hull. Everyone who does not get seasick should do this at least once. Maybe not the Dry Tortugas, but there are other places like the Bahamas or the Caribbean Islands.

Chapter 27.
BASTA/First Trip To Cuba

In the early nineties a group sprang up called BASTA. In Spanish this word means enough.

This group of people wanted to give humanitarian aide to the Cuban people by taking food, medical supplies, and school supplies to the island by boat from Key West. The leader of this group was John Young. He lived in Key West for several years, became interested in the plight of the poor Cubans, and decided to do something about it. He contacted the U.S. Government and got all the information on travel to Cuba. He found there was an embargo, but no travel restrictions. The catch is that Americans can't spend money there. Only the press could spend one hundred dollars per day. I decided to join BASTA and sign up to carry people and some foods on the *Ms. Gina*. I met several authors, reporters, and lawyers that were also interested in this venture. The Miami Herald wanted me to take two people, a reporter and a cameraman, on the boat lift of supplies to Cuba. All the items that we carried were donated. I agreed.

Now I had to find a mate with a passport. I knew several mates: Vance, Victor, and others without passports. Derrick Stirup stood out as a good candidate. His grandfather witnessed my grandfather's will in the Bahamas before they both came to Key West over one hundred years earlier. Derrick usually worked for Johnny Potter, doing day trips as well as Tortugas trips for three or four days at a time. He knew more about long trips than I did, plus he could cook and had a great sense of humor. I could not find anyone with a passport and Derrick had all the other qualifications I was looking for, so he and I talked about the trip with Johnny. He said it would be okay for Derrick to take time off if Derrick found a replacement mate while he went with me.

Derrick and I got busy getting the provisions, checking out the safety equipment with the Coast Guard, and checking the engines. I went to U.S. Customs office. They issued a travel stamp for a fee of $25. The travel stamp is a sticker which must be displayed on the outside of your vessel.

John Young gave us a paper telling us the agenda. Starting on September 4, 1993, we would leave Key West Harbor at eight in the morning. Going on the flotilla would be sail boats, power boats, and a landing craft loaded with goods and fuel. Key West to Havana is ninety miles. We would take a heading of two hundred-ten degrees and the trip should take six to eight hours depending on the stiffness of the current in the gulf stream. The stream travels at a speed of five knots in a northerly direction. It would be against us going to Cuba but in our favor as we returned.

The weather that day was cloudy and overcast with a stiff southeasterly breeze at fifteen miles per hour. My heading of two hundred-ten degrees would cause the vessel to ride in the troughs of the waves and make the boat rock from side to side--not comfortable at all for a long trip, so I changed course to a more southerly one of two hundred degrees. This heading caused the boat to hit the waves at a forty-five degree angle. This makes for a much better ride.

After three hours we got to the gulf stream. I changed course to due west to catch up to the original course and we did a little fishing.

Derrick saw some birds flying and put two sea witch feathers and ballyhoo rigs on the fifty pound rods and reels. The speed we were traveling wouldn't be to fast for tuna, bonita, or wahoo. The young man and woman from the newspaper were inside the cabin, staying dry and out of the wind. Derrick went inside and asked them if they wanted to catch a fish. They were enthusiastic and came on deck. Derrick got them seated in the fighting chairs. As the reporter sat in the chair, an oceanic bonita struck the bait. This fish is in the tuna family. They fight with tenacity and are shaped like a football. She, the reporter, knew nothing about fighting the fish. Derrick is good with the people and calms them down quickly. I slowed the boat down. The lady reeled the fish up to the side of the boat. The mate gaffed the fish and swung it into the fish box. Now is was the guy's turn. I sped up the boat. The two lines were back in the water and we searched for some birds circling. (Find the birds and you find the fish.) In a few minutes the photographer had caught a fish and it was time to get back to the business and join the other boats in the flotilla.

On a trip like this with a large group of different kinds of boats it is impossible to stay together. Each boat travels at a different speed.

Each captain had his own course and he is the boss of his vessel.

The gulf stream is usually thirty miles out of Key West, plus or minus a few miles. It is about thirty miles wide. A while after passing through the stream you can see the coast of Cuba. The tall mountains are on the horizon. You are still twenty-five to thirty miles off the coast.

Before I left to go on this voyage, like always, I went to see Red. I asked how he had navigated to Cuba in the rumrunning days. He used to carry beverages on a speed boat in the 1930's. He said that he would head southwest until the glow of the lights of Key West went out then he would look southwest to see the glow of Havana and go towards them. So much for our modern conveniences like Satellite Navigation, Loran, or GPS.

When we reached Cuban waters, using channel 16 on the VHF radio, we called the Hemingway Marina. We were asked to identify ourselves. We did this and explained we were part of the BASTA flotilla. They acknowledged this and explained how to enter their channel.

Entering Cuba the first time was interesting as well as a little scary. We tied up to the sea wall with three other boats. The Cuban customs, agriculture, and immigration officials go to each vessel. We exchanged greetings, checked passports, and boat papers. Everything was in order except for Derrick. He didn't have a passport. He only had his Florida driver's license. This turned out to be a big problem. The officer in charge said Derrick would have to stay at the Customs Office until the boat left Cuba. I complained quietly, and said I needed a mate to tie up the boat and he had other duties. The officers explained they would have plenty of people at the dock to take care of these things. He said Derrick was staying there with him, along with my 38 Smith & Wesson stainless steel pistol, until we left the country. Derrick protested and said he would stay on the boat. The Cuban Customs Official won the argument and Derrick was taken to the customs lockup until we left. They said the accommodation was nice and he would be fed well.

From the customs house to the designated dock was a short trip at idle speed, so as not to make a wake and disturb the other boats. Sure enough, there were lots of people hanging out, wanting to grab the dock lines and help out.

The Miami Herald reporter and her photographer got off and disappeared into the crowd. I was left with a dirty boat, little fuel, and a language barrier. A middle-aged lady from the welcoming committee came up to me and asked if there was anything she could do for me.

I told her about poor Derrick. She said she would check into the situation. She asked if I was from Key West.

I said, "Yes, and my father was Hemingway's captain there."

She said, "Sanchez, the captain in Cuba is still alive. Would you like to meet him?"

I declined because I had a lot of things to do on the boat to get ready for the return trip.

I offloaded the supplies I had brought and hired two guys to wash the boat. While they were doing that, I took a stroll to see the other boats and people. I met Wayne Kruer, a lawyer from Key West. He was also the legal adviser for BASTA and spoke fluent Spanish. I told him about Derrick. He agreed to meet with me the next morning after the confusion at the dock settled down.

The next morning, Wayne and I went to look for Derrick. Asking questions and walking around, we go to the pool and bar area. There Derrick sat at the bar. Wayne and I went over to see how he was treated the night before. He said everything was fine. He stayed in a small house, the place the guards rested in between boat arrivals and departures. He went on to tell about in the night when he got up to pee, he walked through the living room. Several guards were sleeping in the chairs and on the couch. All of their guns and rifles were lying on the big coffee table in the middle of the room. He quietly went to the bathroom and returned to his room.

Derrick asked me for money to get a few beers and a snack. I gave him one hundred dollars, which was his day's pay. He thought I owed him three hundred dollars. I reminded him he was not working on the boat, he was in jail; such as it was. I reminded him we would be leaving the next day in the afternoon.

The two Miami Herald people I brought over told me they were going to take an airplane back to Miami. This meant I could leave any time I wanted.

I spent the day and night visiting with the boat owners and going to the Tike Bar that night. Boats that were leaving at seven in the morning, awakened me early. After I was up for a while and had had my two cups of coffee in the cockpit, Wayne and another man came up and asked if they could ride back to Key West with me. They had come on another boat that was very crowded.

I said, "No problem." We would be leaving about noon. They put their bags on board and would be ready. I needed fuel. Arrangements had been made for the boats to buy fuel from the marina. The normal price was three dollars a liter but we got it for one dollar a liter, so I got a hundred dollars worth. *Ms. Gina* carries two hundred-twenty gallons. The tank was half full before I got fuel. Because the gulf stream is going with us on the trip back to Key West, it is an easier and faster trip.

Everyone but Derrick was on board. We idled back to the customs house. We had to wait in line because there were other boats leaving. There was no problem getting my gun or Derrick back.

It was only a six-hour ride back. The day was beautiful. There was a light southeast breeze causing long rolling waves. The sky was clear with a few puffy white clouds. The kind of clouds that look like big pillows. After we were underway for three hours, Derrick made a tray of cheese and crackers and cut up luncheon meat and bread. This impressed the passengers. Derrick thought he might get a tip since the guys were riding for free. Unfortunately for him, free was free to the passengers.

Derrick put out the fishing lines, and we followed several weed lines, but no takers.

Back in Key West, we checked in with U.S. Customs. The man checked the boat papers and my captain's license, as well as passports. He also told me Happy Birthday---and so it was!

Chapter 28.
Victor & The Voodoo Charter

Having Victor as a mate is quite an adventure in itself. He has red wiry hair pulled back into a ponytail and white Irish skin that is exposed to the sun most of the time. His build is slight but muscular. The thoughts in his mind come right out of his mouth. Some of these odd comments shock people. Other comments make them laugh.

Vance's Mother, LaNell, came to Key West one winter to visit her son. At the time, he was living with Victor. After she had been there for several days, I saw her at the dock. I asked her what she thought of Victor. She said, "Well, (pause), well (another pause), he is colorful!"

Another time, Carol had gone to the store for supplies for the boat. As she approached the boat with two large brown paper bags in her arms, Victor came out of the cabin and saw her struggling.

The first thing he said was, "Here comes the bag lady!"

Carol replied, "Just take these damn bags, mate!"

One time Victor booked the boat. He called me at home to say he had a one hundred dollar deposit for the next day. It was February and the king fish were snapping.

The next morning I got to the boat a little early. The charter guests hadn't shown up yet. Victor was doing the mate stuff: getting the bait and ice, and checking engines. I am quiet in the morning, so I stowed my gear and went to the bridge and started the engines so they could warm up. A few moments later a van pulled up behind the boat. Six people in white outfits got out and came to the back of the boat. I backed up close to the dock to make it easy for them and Victor gave each person a hand to help them aboard.

As I watched the parties get settled, I wondered why this group of Black Americans were wearing these white outfits, head to toe. I thought this was some kind of group, maybe religious. I knew of a church in Miami called

Yahweh. They wore white clothing and were mostly black people.

When we started out the North West Channel, one of the men came up on the bridge. He sat on one of the benches and asked if he could ask me some questions about the today's trip.

I said, "Yes, if I could ask some questions, too."

He replied, "Sure, that's fair."

He wanted to know the usual things--where we were going, what we were going to catch, how big are the fish going to be, and how deep is the water.

I told the man that at this time of the year, king macherel move south from Texas and Louisiana to seek warm water and food. When this happens the commercial fishermen get airplanes to fly over the waters and find large schools so they can surround them with their nets. We sport fishermen have a two fish per person limit, counting the charter guests, captain, and mate. We were going to go out in the Gulf of Mexico to forty to sixty feet of water and get our limit of king mackerels. They would weigh from ten to forty pounds each.

He said, "That sounds like great fun."

Now it was my turn to ask the questions. I asked why everyone was dressed in white.

He said, "They were of the Voodoo religion. The lady down below is a Voodoo Priestess and the rest of the people are in training."

"Voodoo!"
"Yes, Voodoo."
I asked, "Are you from Haiti?"
He said, "No, from Pennsylvania."
I thought it was time to drop the subject and get on with the fishing trip. I figured I better let well enough alone. I knew little about this religion, only what I saw on TV and movies and none of the facts. It's not a good idea to upset any of these people because of the serious circumstances. I didn't know what might happen.

It takes about the same time to get to the fishing grounds in the gulf as it does in the Atlantic, about forty-five minutes. I never leave the dock until eight o'clock and return at four. This lets other boats that like to get out early locate the fish and tell me where to start. It's nice to have friends on the other boats. When we arrived at the school of mackerel, there were at least fifteen other boats of all sizes already there. Victor put out the lines. Two lines on the outriggers pulled up close because of the number of boats in a small area. Then he let out the flat line and finally let the deep troll line forty feet.

Shortly after the lines were out, we got a strike on the left rigger. Victor quickly grabbed the rod. He gave it to the closest person. The charter started winding. Boom! The right rigger goes down. Victor grabs the rod out of the holder, tightens the slack, and sticks the rod in the gimble of the chair for the next person to start winding. The first guy had a fish on for a while, and then the line went slack. People think the fish are gone, so they quit reeling, but sometimes the fish is swimming towards the boat. That will create slack in the line also. This time the fish was really gone. The fish on the right rigger had the same results. This happened several times so I yelled down to Victor to tighten the drags. He answered that they were tight. I suggested that he loosen them or do something because we were losing too many fish.

Victor replied, "I guess we will have to sacrifice a goat."

The man seated in the big fighting chair said, "Does that work?"

Victor comes back with, "If that doesn't work, we will have to kill a chicken."

I had no clue if Victor knew that these people were Voodoo or not, but I was expecting some kind of reply but the guests gave no response. Boy, was I glad.

The fishing was good and we managed to get our limit. I believe it was two hundred-forty pounds of king mackerel. The charter guests took the filleted fish with them in their coolers.

Chapter 29.
Mr. Garcia & Son, Michael/Trip to Cay Sal Banks

After a few trips to Cuba, I was known as a captain with a boat that would take people to Cuba or on other overnight trips.

In the late summer, when, as Derrick says, "Something has to be done about this dripping." It's time to go to the bar.

This time it was off to the Hookeelou and happy hour. Carol and I were sitting at the bar when one of the mates from the dock came up to me and said that he needed a boat to go looking for some people that had left Cuba trying to get to the United States.

I asked Manny, the mate, "Who is going to pay for this trip?" He had met a Cuban man from Miami who wanted someone to go out and at least look for his relatives. They had left

Cuba and were supposed to be in a little green boat. Manny suggested we go meet the man and his son. They were waiting behind my boat at the dock at City Marina. Carol and I left the Hookeelou. By this time I am a little drunk and it was getting dark.

Two men I did not know and Manny were at the dock when we arrived. We parked behind the boat. Carol and I got out of my pick up and approached these people. I introduced myself as Captain Bud, the owner of the *Ms. Gina*. The gentleman asked what would I charge him to take a trip to look for his relatives that were escaping from Cuba?

I tried to explain that there is a lot of water between the Florida Keys and Cuba and this little boat could be anywhere. He insisted he wanted to do this. I explained, if I did the trip it would go as follows: we would load the *Ms. Gina* with food and water for four people for four days. We would leave Key West and motor to Marathon, fifty miles up the Keys. We would fuel up the boat there and head for the Cay Sal Banks that are located seventy miles east of Marathon. The Cay Sal Banks are a group of islands located at the east end of Cuba. The islands are just big rocks sticking out of the ocean. They are about the size of a super Wal Mart, including the parking lot. In other terms, they are about two or three acres. These islands are part of the Bahamas, not part of Cuba. To enter another country, I should go to the customs entry point of that country and check in and check out. In this case the closest customs check in to the Bahamas is at least another hundred miles away. We were not going to land on the islands, just cruise around looking for his missing relatives, so we would not go through customs. Since these islands are very close to Cuba, many small boats found refuge there. After searching the area we would return to Marathon and then Key West. The price would be one thousand dollars per day and one thousand dollars for the fuel, plus they would bring the food. In other words, it would cost five thousand dollars. On the boat would be Manny as a mate, Carol to navigate and cook, and his son to verify that we covered the search area. I also specified if we found his relatives, we could not let them board my boat. All we could do for them was give them food, water, fuel or medical supplies. This is the law.

Mr. Garcia said, "That sounds good. Let's do it!"

He would give me half the money now and the rest when we returned.

Carol and I went home to get some rest and clothes. We were going to leave at six o'clock in the morning and arrive at Marathon about eleven or twelve. Manny and the son, Michael, were going to get the groceries and sleep on the boat.

Carol was up for another adventure. This trip sounded like fun and a challenge to do some more navigating. She always plots our course on the navigational charts every hour to show our position, time of day, and course heading.

We arrived at the boat at five thirty. Manny and Michael had the groceries stored away, plenty of ice in the chest, and bait in case we ran in to a school of dolphin.

I checked the oil and coolant in the engines, got some extra oil from the dock box, and told Captain Johnny Potter our float plan and when we should return back.

We left Key West on time and arrived in Marathon about eleven. We had no problems or breakdowns so far. While we were fueling up Mr. Garcia arrived in Marathon with a hand pump and plastic barrels for extra fuel. On a long trip like this we needed to carry all the extra fuel that was possible. We had borrowed a hundred-gallon bladder made of rubber that laid across the bow like a water mattress. We tied it to the bow railing stantons so it couldn't slide with the movement of the boat. This trip should be two hundred-forty miles total. Unlike traveling on land in a car the wind and current play an important part in fuel consumption so we wanted to have extra on hand.

Off we go after lunch, saying good-bye to Mr. Garcia. Carol, Manny, Michael, and I start south to look for a small fourteen-foot homemade skiff, painted hunter green. The day was great. A light southeasterly breeze blows like most days of late summer in the keys. We set our course for Dog Rock, Cay Sal Banks, Bahamas. We should reach them before dark. Along the way we find several vessels made of doors, truck inner tubes, and homemade boats. Each one had an orange life jacket or orange paint on them, but no people. A Coast Guard Cutter got within a mile of us and called for me to identify our vessel and explain what we were doing there.

I replied, "*Ms. Gina* from Key West with four people including the captain and crew. We are fishing." They went away.

We arrived at Dog Rocks just before dark. It was time to anchor the boat, eat dinner, and fish a little before turning in for the night. Sleeping on a boat is difficult for me. If I sleep below decks in the stateroom or v-birth it is very hot unless the generator is running the air conditioning, and you hear the waves slapping the side of the hull. We were conserving fuel, so we did not run the generator. Sleeping on the fly bridge is okay if the weather cooperates and does not rain, dew, or storm. When the tide changes, the boat will swing to a new direction. This will cause me to wake up. The weather cooperated this night, but I still slept lightly.

Waking up at first light, we had coffee and pulled the anchor. We continued to head south looking for the small green skiff. Soon after taking off, a small jet airplane scraffs us. The colors on the plane indicate it is a Coast Guard plane. Soon after the noise of the jet cleared, the radio started talking on Channel 16, the international initial contact channel.

"*Ms. Gina, Ms. Gina, Ms, Gina.* This is the U.S. Coast Guard, Channel 16."

I replied with the same message as I had before. We were from Key West, had four people on board, and were fishing.

The answer from the Coast Guard was, "Have a good day!"

I have the wheel. I am watching the depth finder closely. The charts say the depth, but unless the water is over fifty feet I still stay alert. This is another beautiful day. The sky is clear. The sun is hot. The crystal clear water is unbelievable. You can almost see the bottom at the depth of fifty feet. On days like this, I can't believe people are paying me to ride around on my own boat and having a great time.

Years ago in my father's day a lot of Key West fishermen came here for a week at a time, but not any more. As we cruised the waters, we saw a few rafts floating in the water, always with a life jacket or orange paint on them. This was done to indicate the Coast Guard had retrieved the passengers off the rafts and they were taken on the Coast Guard vessel. I learned this in one of the conversations with the Coast Guard. I maintained a speed of ten to twelve knots till we arrived at the last island which had a small sand beach. We see two or three small craft on the beach. Because of the shallow depth about two hundred yards off the beach is as close as the *Ms. Gina* could get. With the binoculars we can see that all the boats have the orange signs on them. Continuing on our quest, we head north on the other side of the islands. I can see a large ship to the west of me. Also, I see Cuba to the west. A small Zodiac inflatable boat with two Coast Guard men on board comes over to see us. They ask the same questions and we give the same answers. We continue on back towards Dog Rock to make sure we covered all the small rock islands in the Cay Sal Banks area. We did not see the green boat on any of the islands. We headed back to the gulf stream and on to Marathon. On the way back, every now and then, we would see a boat or homemade raft. All of them had the orange markings so we knew the Coast Guard had retrieved the people.

Late that afternoon was the last time the Coast Guard came close to investigate us. Carol had left the bridge to check our location and estimate our time of arrival in Marathon. The same *Ms. Gina, Ms. Gina, Ms. Gina,* the same questions, with the same answer, only this time I said we were headed for Marathon. I asked how far was it and what was our present location? There was silence for a few minutes. Then they replied with their location. I said thanks and we were on our way again. Soon Carol came out of the cabin. I told her the location that they had given me. Nevertheless, using Carol's information, we arrived in Marathon close to dark and spent the night at the marina with electric to run the air conditioning so I could get a good night's sleep.

Michael called his father who lived about seventy-five miles away. He would see us in the morning. Over brunch we told him the story of our trip. I was paid the rest of the money. Manny, Carol, and I headed back to Key West. Upon arriving at my dock at City Marina we encountered a lot of law enforcement people. The U.S. Customs Agents, the Border Patrol

Officer, the Department of Agriculture Agent, the Federal Fisheries Agent, and the Key West City Police were there to greet us. The only ones not present were the Sheriff's Department. As soon as the boat was tied to the dock, all these people started talking to me. The City Police handcuffed Manny and put him under arrest. The Customs people wanted to fine me for not calling them when I arrived. A Border Patrol Officer asked to inspect the boat, which I agreed to. Manny was hauled off. Then I got mad and loud and asked the police why this was happening. They ignored me. In a few minutes things settled down. The Border Patrol was satisfied I had no stowaways from Cuba and they left. The City Police took Manny away. One of the detectives was left to ask questions about Manny. Carol started removing luggage and supplies from the boat to the pickup. On one of her trips to the truck she was carrying an armload of guns. She had a Winchester thirty-thirty, a twelve gauge Remington shotgun, a sixteen gauge Ithaca double-barreled shotgun and a Smith & Wesson thirty-eight revolver, plus a box of shell for each. Before getting to the truck the detective for the City approached her and started asking questions about our trip and what Manny was doing there. She explained the trip and that Manny was the fishing mate and that was all we knew. After the interrogation, she put all the weapons into the front seat of the truck. The police officer said nothing about the guns or if they were registered. He just turned and walked away.

Meanwhile, back in my interrogation room, the salon of the boat, I was asked about where we had been and why and did we bring back any fish? If so, on what side of the imaginary line that separated the U.S. Waters from the Bahamian waters we had caught them. I answered we did not bring back any fish from the Bahamas and I didn't know there was a line separating the U.S. Fish from the Bahamian fish. The Federal Fisheries man was satisfied and he left.

The only ones left were the U.S. Customs Officials. A nice young man in his mid thirties did all the writing. A dishwater blonde woman with a authoritarian attitude asked the questions. The officer filling out the forms took our passports. We were asked when we had left Key West and where we had been. I told her Marathon, Fl., to Cay Sal Banks and back. I also explained that we remained on the boat the entire time from Marathon to Cay Sal Banks and back to Marathon.

The officer asked, "How do I know this is the truth?"

I bring out the yellow legal pad and the navigation chart, which has our position recorded for the entire trip. This satisfies him but not the female officer. She wants to fine us for something.

The male officer is filling out his form and he writes down my date of birth and says, "Happy Birthday, Bud!"

A few weeks later I get a letter from U.S. Customs saying they are fining me five thousand dollars for failing to call customs upon returning to the United States. After our lawyer had some discussions with Customs Officers at the district level, the charges were dropped.

Chapter 30.
Good Bye To The Captain

On March 24, 1996, the Key West Citizen reported in the obituary column that a long time Key Wester had passed away. There were a few lines stating the names of the relatives and that Red Williams had once been Ernest Hemingway's boat captain. His date of birth, July 14, 1909, and date of death, March 23, 1996, were also stated.

A man lives, works, gets married, had children, and so on for eighty-five years. It was condensed into a few lines in the newspaper or "mullet wrapper" as Red called it.

So now I'm going to tell you how I made a big tado out of his funeral to celebrate his life.

When I was in my preteen years I saw funerals in Key West put on by the black population. They had a brass band that walked from the mortuary to the graveyard. They were all dressed in black, a dozen band members along with forty or fifty mourners. The band played slow music, sang hymns, and they walked in cadence, stepping together like an army would do in a slow parade. After walking to the graveyard and completing the ceremony, the group paraded back to the church. This time the music was fast and joyful. The mourners were no longer sad. They clapped their hands and sang at the top of their lungs.

I was interested in doing something like this for Red. I asked a black city councilman if this was possible. It could be done but it would take a lot of planning and permits now.

This wouldn't work. Red had said that he wanted to be buried at sea in the Gulf Stream so he would return every five years because the stream makes a complete circle every five years.

I devised a plan. I had an old wooden sea trunk, the American flag he received from the VA, and several newspaper articles published in the Key West Citizen that I had saved over the years. I made a shrine in the bed of my new Mark III, Ford pickup. Carol, Vance, and I took Red's ashes from bar to bar: Red's Place, The Bull, The Schooner Wharf, etc. At each place Red's friends gathered around the truck drinking, reading the articles, and reminiscing about times and life of Red. This lasted from about ten in the morning till eight in the evening.

The next day it was time to take "The Captain" to sea for the last time. It would be the only time that Red, Vance, and I ever took a boat trip together and wouldn't you know it, Vance was an hour late. It wasn't so bad. The extra time gave everyone time to have a beer and reflect on old times.

Captain Curly Spaulding, my mortician friend, had asked months before when Red was sick, if he could prepare a eulogy. Vance and I would sprinkle the ashes and Carol would point the boat into the wind.

It was a cool day, partly cloudy, wind blowing out of the southeast at fifteen knots. This made the ride bumpy for the twenty guests on board.

The trip was going to take about two and a half hours out and back from the deep water. An hour and a half into the trip the sun came out bright and clear. Eight or ten porpoise came to the stern of the *Ms. Gina* to ride the wake. They stayed for a while, then left as fast as they appeared. Shortly after that it was time to do the service. Curly said the words, Vance and I sprinkled the ashes, and some tears were shed. Carol came about and set a course for Key West.

On the return trip some more porpoises came to ride the wake. I took it, and some of the others commented that the porpoises approve and would take good care of Red.

Chapter 31.
Key West Changed and So Did I

After Red, my father and the one everyone called the captain, died things started changing for me.

In the last dozen years becoming part of his world was important to me. I wanted him to know his grandchildren Vance and Gina. He did get to be around them for a while. My son, Vance, lived in Key West and worked on the charter boats like his father and grand father. He also got to see how the life style was and still is for the fisherman. My daughter, Gina, came to visit a few times but never lived in Key West. She stayed in west Texas where she was born and her mother lives.

For me, I got to learn my way around the island. People still lived in the same small conch houses they occupied in the twenties. Red played with the Ramos children in Fort Zachary Taylor and the down town streets that are still there. The Ramos children and I became friends when Red and I worked for them in the eighties.

I got to fish in the waters he fished and go to the bars he went to when he was a young man walking the streets of Key West. I feel so lucky to have been able to take off from the real world to see how people lived, worked, loved, and drank in the small island in the sun amidst the sand, palm trees, and gulf stream.

The changes I mentioned were gradual. At the City Marina, where I docked the *Ms. Gina*, the rent grew by fifty percent. The city made it mandatory to have one million dollars liability insurance. The fee for garbage doubled so the Charter Boat Association raised hell. The city decided not to raise the rate but only give one garbage can to two boats. We ended up with no raise in rates but half the service. It became a constant battle to make any money.

When I first got there each boat had a rack that they hung the day's catch on. The tourists could drive by and see what was being caught. Some people would come by and book a fishing trip and others just drove by to see the big fish. This practice had been going on for years. The city decided to take the racks down.

The state passed a law that banned nets so it became harder and more expensive to get ballyhoo, the bait we used. They also passed more and more laws about what kind of fish we could catch, and how many fish of each species we could posses. To circumvent the law we would catch and release the fish so our customers had some action for their bucks. Most of those fish will probably die anyway, so that practice sounded dumb to me.

Because our costs were going up most of the charter boats had to raise their rates. Also, in the mid nineties booking booths popped up. These are small stalls along Duval Street where people could sign up for fishing, snorkeling, scuba diving, and sailing trips to the reef. These booths took twenty percent off the top. The tourists no longer needed to come to see the boats at the City Marina to book a fishing trip. Besides, there was nothing to see any longer because the racks that displayed the fish were gone.

The Internet became more popular so people could book a charter and not even see the boat or the captain. Money became a big factor. The customers had to pay more so they compared rates from one boat to another boat, not taking into consideration the size of the boat or the experience of the captain. In my early days this business was about fishing. When the boats would back into their slip people were stacked up waiting to see what the days catch was. The mate would wash down the dock and then throw the fish up. Two or three men held out one hundred dollar bills to secure a charter for the next day. They did not even ask the price. This happened most often between Christmas and New Years when the island was full of tourists.

Believe it or not, even the Super Bowl affects the charter fishing business now. When the playoff games moved from mid January to February people stayed home till after the games were played. We lost four weeks of good business.

During the early eighties, drug money was moving freely. The people just wanted to have a good time, maybe even catch a fish. They brought lots of food, beer, alcohol, cocaine, and pot. After the eight hour trip was over they left the food and beer but never the cocaine or pot. They tipped generously and were pleasant to be with.

In the nineties the dot com people came with their credit cards that bounced. Sometimes I had to run as many as three cards to get one that would accept the charges. This new type of charter demanded to catch a blue marlin or a sailfish on a half day trip. I tried to explain what it takes to catch either of these fish but no one ever listened. Reducing the rate was also a big topic of conversation. After booking a charter many of them would spend most of the day telling me how much money they had and how they were going to take care of the mate and captain at the end of the day, which they never did. One afternoon I had a man show up to ask about a trip. He had seven people and wanted a half day. I explained we could only take six people. It was the law made by the US Coast Guard. He asked if I could get another boat and each boat take half of the group. I checked with a few boats left at the dock and none were available. He decided to send the ladies shopping, so we only had five people. After getting underway, I saw we had a young boy about twelve and an older gentleman in his sixties. The guy that booked the boat was in his mid forties. He was well dressed and had a Rolex President. This is a gold Rolex with diamonds around the bezel worth about twenty thousand dollars. I thought there will be no money problems here. As we made our way out the mate lowered the out riggers so they would not hit the two bridges we go under as we head to Key West harbor. During this time the man told me what he wanted to catch, how we were going to do it three times. Each time he made a statement I tried to explain what I was going to do because of the limited amount of time. It takes forty-five minutes to get to the reef and forty-five minutes back, that is one and a half hours. With only two and a half hours of fishing time I was going to stop at the reef and let the boy and older gentleman catch a fish first. After that we will go to deeper water for the remaining time available.

He said, "No! I want to use light tackle and catch a sailfish." I explained again we didn't have enough time on a half day trip. He came back again with his demands. We were both standing on the fly bridge next to each other getting ready for trouble.

I yelled to the mate, "Keep the riggers down, we're going back in." The man climbed down to the cockpit and asked the mate what was wrong? The mate said he was just following the orders of the captain. When we returned to the dock I gave the man back his one hundred dollar deposit and told him there was not enough time to do what he wanted to do.

Not all charters were this way. I saw that people were coming to the boats wanting more fish for less money. I couldn't control the fish or lower the price and stay in business. All I wanted to do is make a living and have fun while I was doing it.

I was in Key West in the mid eighties when Mel Fisher discovered the mother load of treasure on the Atocha, a Spanish ship that sailed from South America in the early sixteen hundreds. It was sunk on the reef about twenty miles west of Key West by a hurricane. He had been looking for years to locate it. This wreck gave up thousands of silver coins called pieces of eight, along with gold coins and silver bars. Many people in Key West had been working for Mel for years and instead of getting paid for their work they received shares in the treasure. When the treasure was found the divers were treasure rich but still cash poor. Because these people still needed pay their rent, many coins were being sold well below their real value. I bought one of the silver coins from my fair-haired bartender at The Bull. Her nickname was Skunk. She had several coins for sale. One afternoon after a morning half day trip I went to The Bull to have a few beers. Skunk brought out her coins and passed them around to see if anyone would like to buy one. I asked how much she was asking.

She said, "Four hundred dollars."

I reached in my pocket and pulled out four hundred-twenty dollars. I slapped it down on the bar and said, "take it all."

After I bought the coin I gave it to a jeweler friend to put a gold bezel with two dolphins around the outside and a loop to hang from a gold chain. During this time many people were making jewelry out of the coins and they became fondly known as Key West dog tags.

After my coin was done and I was wearing it a funny incident happened to me at another local bar, the Schooner Wharf. Seated near me were two couples. The women asked if they could see my coin. I took it off and let the ladies look. Then the larger man in his mid forties got up and took a hold of it and inspected it thoroughly. He asked if it came from the Atocha.

I said, "Yes and I have the authentication papers."

The tourist asked, "How much I would sell it for?"

He started naming numbers, "Five hundred?"

I said, "No."

"Seven fifty?"

"NO."

He said, "I'll trade my watch for your coin and chain?"

I said, "No, I have a good watch and showed him my Tag Heuer.

He showed me the watch on his wrist and said, "You won't trade for my gold Rolex?"

I said, "No!" At that point I went to the other side of the bar and ordered another beer.

I started thinking about what was happening to me and the charter boat business. I had accomplished all the things I wanted to do and more.

I came to Key West to be around my dad to see what kind of person he was and what kind of life he lived and why he didn't pay much attention to me. When I was growing up he never sent a card, money, or even made a phone call. Every five years or so he would pop up in Miami or I would see him in Key West. I remember the time I was playing high school football for Hialeah High and we went to play in Key West. Red was there cheering for me and we won. I learned that he just lived his life day to day just like every one else. I learned you can only control a few things and he was doing what he could.

I learned how to fish, got my captain's license, bought a boat on Charter Boat Row, then a bigger boat. I got to fish the Gulf Stream, go to Cuba several times with BASTA, and other groups of people. Even the Miami Herald called me from time to time to take the press out to cover news events about Cuba.

I realized what I could do yesterday I could not do today. There were more laws restricting the fishing as well as on the island. The bars started closing at two in the morning instead of four, not that anyone needs to drink for those extra two hours but it's a change. There were more stop lights, more condo's, more traffic, and a noise ordinance was passed because people bought houses close to the bars that had loud music.

When my father ran the *Evelyn* during the thirties and forties there were only eight charter boats, now there are over one hundred.

Carol and I took a driving vacation the summer of nineteen ninety-four, the same year Red died. We mapped out a trip all over Georgia starting at Valdosta, then north to Vienna for the Big Pig Gig, and north to Warm Springs where President Roosevelt spent some time. After that we went east stopping at small log cabins for sale. We talked about what a different life it would be if we had some land and a log cabin in the woods with no people, no noise, and fewer laws. We discussed the pros and cons of a move like this. We could get an old travel trailer and place it on our land to see if we liked the woods since it was so different from the Keys. Maybe we could try it for the hot summer months. By the time we had gone north again and reached Blue Ridge, Georgia, we were primed. A real estate agent took us to a mountain top to see some land and Carol said it was too high in the air and in price. The agent asked what she really wanted.

Carol answered, "I want a place where I can walk my dogs and have a stream running through it."

He said, "I have the place." We went off to the woods. This place is fifteen miles from town and two miles off the paved road. After looking around and seeing the cold water stream that crossed the twenty acres, she decided to buy the property because land is a good investment even if we didn't stay there forever.

The next season came and went. I had a few real good trips, such as the charter with the father and two young girls. The girls were about twelve and fourteen. They were big enough to handle anything up to a small marlin. We didn't catch a lot of fish but what we did catch was quality. One girl caught a small sailfish. The other landed a nice thirty pound wahoo.

In discussions at parties, bars, and other gatherings we had from time to time a lot of my friends were talking about moving from Key West to other places. My first captain, Michael Lewis moved to Nevada to teach school. Jimmy Mantz and his wife, Susan, moved to Kentucky to be closer to her mother. Vance met a girl while working on the charter boat *Fishbuster*.

She was the owner's sister. They lived in Albany, New York. After several months of three hundred dollar phone bills, he moved north and got married.

By this time it was nineteen ninety-six. Carol and I decided to sell our house in Key West. It was worth a lot more money now than it was when we bought it. In the summer of ninety-six we built a log cabin on our property in the mountains of North Georgia. We would spend the winters and spring in Key West and the summers and fall in Georgia. I still had the *Ms. Gina* and the dock at the City Marina. I could lease her to one of several captains to pay for the dock rent and utilities for the summer and fall.

The next winter came, time to go back to Key West and haul the boat, paint the bottom, and make her ready for the season that starts December 25 through Memorial Day.

We rented a trailer house while looking for something to buy. We needed something small and cheap. We found a place that was nasty and falling down but we knew how to fix up buildings. This would be our fourth house to repair or build. We called it the giggle house because every time we saw the place Carol laughed. In a few months giggle house was finished. We moved in and had an open house party to show the few friends we had left where we lived. The house was twenty miles north of Key West on Sugarloaf Key.

I got reacquainted with some people I knew in Key West. They had moved up the keys to get cheaper rent. Still I found from time to time that arrogant rich person that tried to impress me with how much money he had. I didn't care how much money he had, I care how much money I had.

After that winter we went to Georgia and rented giggle house for a while. Then a hurricane came through the keys leaving a lot of damage to the area. We decided to sell the giggle house and the boat and stay in Georgia. And to paraphrase a great author, "To hell with all that." No, truthfully it has been a great life so far and there is not much I would change. There is more to come, but for now....

The End.

GLOSSARY

A
ABOARD-On or within the boat.
ABOVE DECK-On the deck.
AFT-Toward the stern of the boat.
AGROUND-touching or fast to the bottom.
AHEAD-In a forward direction.
ANCHORAGE-A place suitable for anchoring in relation to the wind, sea, and bottom.
ASTERN-In back of the boat, opposite of ahead.

B
BACKING DOWN-Operating the boat in reverse while the angler has a fish on the line to help.
BEAM-The greatest width of the boat.
BELOW-Beneath the deck.
BILGE-The interior of the hull below the floor boards.
BILLFISH-Swordfish, Marlin, Spearfish, and Sailfish make up the group. In these fish the upper jaw, or snout is greatly extended. That snout is called a bill.
BOTTOM FISHING-When bottom fishing, the boat is anchored. Usually chum is used to attract fish. bait is then fished at various depths, not necessarily on the bottom. Grouper, snappers, and jack are frequently found at the bottom.

BOW-The forward part of the boat.

BRIDGE-The location from which a vessel is steered and its speed controlled.

BRIDLE-A line or wire secured at both ends in order to distribute a strain between two points.

BRIGHTWORK-Varnished woodwork and/or polished metal.

C

CABIN-A compartment for passengers or crew.

CAST OFF-To let go.

CHART-A map for use by navigators.

CHARTER BOAT-Charter boats are boats that an angler can hire for a day of fishing. Charter boats take a limited number of anglers, usually six.

COCKPIT-An opening in the deck from which the boat is handled.

COURSE-The direction in which a boat is steered.

CURRENT-The horizontal movement of water.

D

DECK-A permanent covering over compartment, hull, or any part thereof.

DINGY-A small open boat. A dingy is often used as a tender for a larger craft.

DOCK-A protected water area in which vessels are moored. The term is often used to denote a pier or wharf.

DOWNRIGGER-A heavy weight, and the reel line to raise and lower the weight. The weight has a clip that holds the fishing line from the reel to the bait. The weight is lowered to the depth one wants to fish, and the downrigger reel is locked. when a fish takes the bait, the clip releases the fishing line and the fish is fought without additional weights that would be needed to get the bait deep. Someone had to reel the weight up so the fish can't tangle the line.

DRAFT-The depth of water the boat draws.

E

EBB-A receding current.

F

FATHOM-Six feet.

FLATS FISHING-Fishing in very shallow water. usually involves spotting a fish by sight and casting a lure or bait in his path.

FORWARD-Toward the bow of the boat.

G

GALLEY-The kitchen area of a boat.

GEAR- General term for ropes, blocks, tackle, and other equipment.

H

HEAD-A marine toilet.

HEADING-The direction in which a vessel's bow points at any given time.
HEADWAY-The forward motion of a boat.
HELM-The wheel or tiller controls the rudder.
HULL-The main body of a vessel.

I

J

K

KEEL-The centerline of a boat running fore and aft: the backbone of a vessel.
KNOT-A measure of speed equal to one nautical mile (6076 feet) per hour.

L

LINE-Rope and cordage used aboard a vessel.
LOG-A record of courses or operation.

M

N

NAUTICAL MILE-One minute of latitude approximately 6,076 feet-about 1/8 longer than the statute mile of 5,280 feet.
NAVIGATION RULES-The regulations governing the movement of vessels in relation to each other, generally called steering and sailing rules.

O

OUTRIGGER-A long pole reaching up and out from the side or stern of a fishing boat. It has near its end a clip which holds the line from the reel to the bait. When a fish strikes the bait, the clip releases the line. Two purposes are served by the outrigger. Several outrigger poles may be placed at various angles allowing several lines to be put in the water without becoming tangled. Second, some bill fish will strike the bait and then circle back to eat it. That strike frees the line from the outrigger and gives the fisherman a signal to release more line so the bait stays where the game fish expects to find it.

P

PIER-A loading platform extending at an angle from the shore.

PORT-The left side of a boat looking forward. A harbor.

Q

QUARTERING SEA-Sea coming at a forty-five degree angle from a boat's bow.

R

RODE-The anchor line and/or chain.

RUDDER-A vertical plate or board for steering a

boat.

S

SCREW-A boat's propeller.

SEAWORTHY-A boat or boat's gear able to meet the usual sea conditions.

STARBOARD-The right side of a boat when looking forward.

STERN-The after part of the boat.

STOW-To put an item in its proper place.

T

TIDE-The periodic rise and fall of water level in the ocean.

TOPSIDES-The sides of a vessel between the waterline and the deck; sometimes referring to or above the deck.

TRANSOM-The stern cross-section of a square sterned boat.

TROLLING-Dragging bait through the water while the boat is moving.

U

UNDERWAY-Vessel in motion, i.e., when not moored, at anchor, or aground.

V

W

WAKE-Moving waves, track or path that a boat leaves behind it, when moving across the water.

WEED LINES-Seaweed will frequently drift in large windows on the surface of the water. The weed lines provide cover for bait fish, while attracting game fish.

X

Y

Z

Sport Fishing Boat

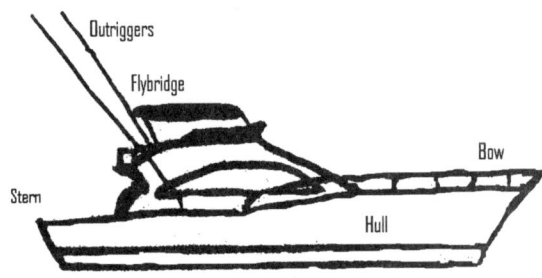

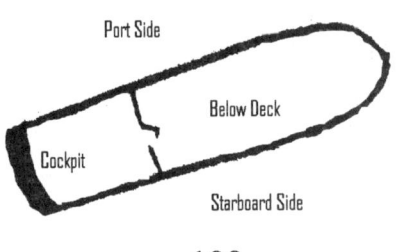

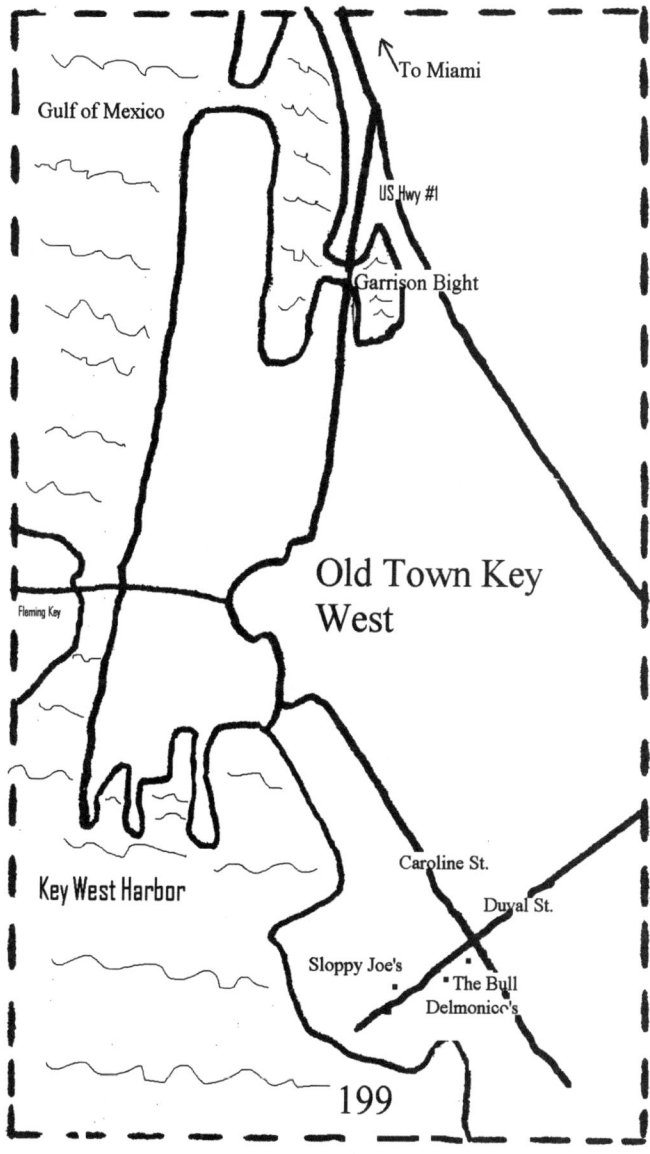

Florida Straights